9-26
10-19

A

OSLG
F
10-06

I1032068

SEP   2006

Guns Up

**Center Point
Large Print**

**This Large Print Book carries the
Seal of Approval of N.A.V.H.**

Guns Up

ERNEST HAYCOX

CENTER POINT PUBLISHING
THORNDIKE, MAINE

This Center Point Large Print edition
is published in the year 2006 by arrangement with
Golden West Literary Agency.

Copyright © 1928 by Doubleday, Doran & Co., Inc.
Copyright © renewed 1955 by Jill Marie Haycox.

All rights reserved.

The text of this Large Print edition is unabridged. In other
aspects, this book may vary from the original edition. Printed in
Thailand. Set in 16-point Times New Roman type.

ISBN 1-58547-807-5

Library of Congress Cataloging-in-Publication Data

Haycox, Ernest, 1899-1950.
    Guns up / Ernest Haycox.--Center Point large print ed.
        p. cm.
    ISBN 1-58547-807-5 (lib. bdg. : alk. paper)
    1. Large type books. I. Title.

PS3515.A9327G86 2006
813'.52--dc22

2006004103

Western
Haycox, Ernest, 1899-1950.
Guns up [large print]

1. The Champifer—Boadley feud

On this blazing hot day—so hot that the surrounding
prairie quivered under the successive layers of heat and
the not far distant Medical Peak was bereft of snow up
to its very tip—history was definitely repeating itself in
the isolated cattle town of Grail City. This morning the
Champifer clan gathered along the half of the street to
the west of White River, walking sullen and fretful on
its chosen ground, as it had walked thus for better than
thirty years; while across the stream, no wider at this
point than an irrigation ditch, the Boadleys quietly
watched their ancient adversaries. Even the scarred and
paint-peeled buildings seemed to share that feud, the
two rows facing each other over the dividing strip with
a settled grimness. Even the faded signs added to the
challenge forever resting upon the two halves of the
county. On the Champifer side stood a hotel with this
sign: "Old Grail City House." Almost directly opposite,
on the Boadley bank of the sluggish stream was
another hotel bearing upon its pine paneling a stinging
retort, "Grail City House—Not Old Enough to be Full
of Bugs, But the Pioneer Hostelry of Grail County."

Grail County took its feud seriously. There were no
known neutrals; men were enlisted under one banner or
the other. And from the very conformation of the
county, none possibly could be neutral. White River,
rising in the Medical Range to northward, divided the
county in approximately equal portions as it meandered

5

south and sank beneath the porous sands of the John Despard Sinks. To west was Champifer range, every inch of it; to east was the empire of the Boadleys. The ancestral roots of these factions went far back into the Indian fighting days and because of their power and foresight no lesser outfits had ever gained an acre within the county boundaries. Nothing happened in Grail without warrant of authority from either a Champifer or a Boadley. As to the original cause of the quarrel, few men knew it, and none cared. It might have arisen over a gambling debt, or it might have been the natural friction of two strong clans placed together—too near together. The Champifers were ambitious people and good haters. The Boadleys were content to let well enough alone, yet would brook no infringement of rights.

Ordinarily, Grail City was a drowsy place, tucked in a remote section of the state and subsisting entirely upon the trade of the factions. There were two of everything, one on each side of the river: a store for a Champifer and a store for a Boadley, and thus down the line. A narrow wooden bridge linked the halves, but, save on specified occasions, a man of either faction would as soon be shot dead as to enter the opposite territory. So it went, ordinarily. There was a grumbling peace, made uneasy by the subterranean fires of feud. Nevertheless it was peace. There had been no overt hostility since the last great flaring war fifteen years back, the war which left so many dead men that the head of each clan had agreed to a truce and drawn up

6

formal rules for future conduct. And, with the memory of death and destruction still fresh in their minds, they had vowed the peace must be kept.

Today was one of those specified occasions. Today was election time. A Champifer had been sheriff the preceding two years. It was now time for a Boadley to assume the office, according to the rules of the truce. And precisely at ten o'clock of this sweltering morning, three riders disengaged themselves from the restless tide of men and moved toward the bridge—two coming from the Champifer side and one from the Boadley side. They met in the middle of the bridge, and as they entered upon the parley every eye in town bent upon them.

The head of the Champifers was Old Pierre, a shrunken figure of a man as swart as any Indian and sitting like an Indian in his saddle, humped over, toes pointing out. He had the Champifer stamp all over him—intensely black and flashing a curved nose, and high bulging cheek muscles, the heritage of early Gallic blood. His was a character formed out of turbulence. It was easy to guess he had bitterly disciplined tempestuous emotions, and that on occasion those emotions might yet flare up and get the best of him. The man beside him, younger by a full thirty years, was enough in likeness to be a son. Yet Nuck Champifer was a nephew and of all the Champifer tribe the most sullen and turbulent and ill-bridled. He was, in fact, an exact picture of what Old Pierre Champifer might have been in youth. Nuck's under lip fell away slackly. Restlessness would not let him be still. And when he stared at Lone Star Boadley, it was in the manner of a man daring another to strike.

As for Lone Star Boadley, he towered head and shoulders above the Champifers. He sat like a cavalryman and from the crown of his Stetson to his boot heels he represented bulk and evenness of disposition. It was he who raised his hand first by way of greeting. It was he who first broke the silence, inclining his head courteously toward both the Champifers.

"Glad to see you gentlemen again. Powerful warm day."

Nuck Champifer grunted. He seemed about to blurt out a short and spiteful retort. Old Pierre suppressed him with a sharp glance, the meanwhile answering Lone Star Boadley. "Yes, sir, it's hot. Our range is burning up. We will have to shift to the upper pastures earlier this season. My men tell me White River is going dry at the Sinks. I will send a man to ride there."

"I shall do the same," replied Lone Star.

This, too, was a part of the rules of truce. White River was the dividing line of their respective ranges. In summer its trickle of water sank below the ground at the Sinks and this raised the barrier that held Champifer and Boadley stock from mixing. And each season a man of each faction was stationed by the river to prevent that straying and its consequent ill-will.

"This being the time for a Boadley election," Lone Star pursued gravely, "I assume it we will hold the vote on our side of town. I have designated Markowitz's store as the polling place. My son Snass will be clerk for us."

"I shall appoint my brother, Luke Only, to represent us in that capacity," Old Pierre said. "I have, all told, fifty men in town. Nuck here will be our candidate. As the usual matter of form I will instruct one half of my party to vote for him. The others I will have vote for your candidate. It is the agreement, is it not?"

"It is the agreement," Lone Star replied. "Were it not for possible state intervention or outside public opinion I have thought it might be simpler to let each election go by default. In your term I wouldn't set up an opposing candidate; in our term you would not set up a candidate. But perhaps we had better go through with the usual rigmarole for sake of appearances."

"It is best," Old Pierre declared, "to keep up appearances. Otherwise some down-state reformer might raise a kick. Not that it would do him any good, yet it is best to keep all public attention off this county. So long as I command my men and you command yours, the agreement cannot be broken."

Lone Star nodded. "The voting will start at one o'clock then. Your men will vote first. My men will stay out of the road until you are all finished and away."

"Whom are you running?" Old Pierre asked.

"My son Allan," Lone Star said. And for the first time a slight line broke the even serenity of his countenance. It was the custom of these two leaders, each time they met on the bridge to arrange the election, to bring with them the candidate they had chosen. Old Pierre had for this reason brought Nuck. Lone Star came alone and it disturbed him to vary the accustomed procedure; for as much as each disliked the other, neither of the elder men would brook an infraction of the peace. They had seen the bloody results of a war. They had in fact led the last war, and they were determined it should never happen again. They clung tenaciously to every dot and comma of their agreement, they were scrupulously exact. "I'd have brought him with me," Lone Star added, "but he's off traveling in the Medical Range again. Fact is, he doesn't know he's to be the next sheriff. You understand this."

"It doesn't make the least difference," Old Pierre said, inclining his head. "Very well. I will lead my men across at one o'clock, see them vote and bring them back. Half will vote for Nuck, the rest for your son Allan. That will be plenty to swing it?"

"Ample," Lone Star agreed. "I'm away short of a full crew this season or it would not be necessary for you to switch any of your votes."

"I bid you good day," said Old Pierre, bowing a second time.

Lone Star raised his hat. They turned and rode back to their respective sides. And such was the inflammable quality of the moment, and such the temper of rank and file, that neither Lone Star Boadley nor Old Pierre Champifer had ventured to vary the set and polite gravity of their features during the interview, or dared to look backward as they rode off the bridge.

The sullen and slack-lipped Nuck Champifer owned

no such scruples. Being afraid of Old Pierre—as other Champifers were—he held his tongue during the parley. But scarcely had this terminated when he began to grumble beneath his breath and to sow his restless and moody glances through the Champifer crew and all other Champifer partisans in town. Old Pierre affected not to see this. He dropped from the saddle in front of the hotel and went inside, Nuck following closely. Here waited the rest of the immediate family—Luke Only, Little William and Susan, along with a pair of Champifer foremen. Nuck could no longer contain himself. All the outraged pride flamed forth in one tempestuous interjection.

"I'm damned if I'll be a dummy candidate. I'll play no second fiddle to any Boadley, let alone that lumbering elephant of an Allan! You hear me, Uncle Pierre?"

"You will obey my instructions," Old Pierre said crisply. "This peace is going to be kept."

"I'm sick of hearing about the peace," Nuck grumbled. "It's an old gag. What's the use of us voting in a Boadley? Keep the crew solid and I'll get the job— we'll have it in the family another two years. It's all a pack of foolishness, this toadying to them folks. Why, they can't muster half our numbers! They're on the downhill grade. They're running a bluff on you, that's what it amounts to. We got a plain majority. Have had one for six years. We ought to run this county for keeps."

"They may be less in numbers," said Old Pierre,

dropping into a chair, "but that doesn't affect their fighting ability. You were a small lad, Nuck, when the last war took place. You have no idea what such a thing is like. Whether they are fewer than us or whether they are greater—it's of no consequence. We've got an agreement. It's worked for fifteen years. I'm repeating, Nuck, we'll abide by the rules."

"Some day—" Nuck muttered. He stopped suddenly, for Old Pierre's jet black eyes were playing on him. All the hard and suppressed fury of the elder's nature flashed up to the surface, flamed a moment, and was gone. "Be about your business, Nuck," said Old Pierre. His head ducked toward Luke Only and he issued his orders in the manner of one whose will had never been questioned. "Luke, you'll represent us at the voting booth. Now, go out and tell twenty-five of the boys to drop a cross opposite Allan Bradley's name. Understand?"

Luke Only moved across the room, taller than the rest of the Champifers, older even than his brother Old Pierre. There was a resemblance between them, but none other of the family had the withered sourness of face he possessed, and none was so unkept. He had fought beside Old Pierre in the last range war. He had the same memory of swift destruction and of free-flowing blood. Yet being a more calloused man, more given to nursing his dislikes, he had not learned the lesson of it. Willingly he would have gone into the street and challenged the Boadley clan to reopen the issue. Old Pierre well understood it, and perhaps for that reason he held a short rein on Luke Only as well as on Luke Only's two sons, Nuck and Little William.

Luke Only nodded and walked out of the door. On the threshold he glanced backward, at which Nuck and Little William followed. The two foremen likewise ambled after, leaving Old Pierre alone with Susan. The man's face sagged a little; worry crept between his eyes. "We are going to have trouble, my girl. I crack the whip over those three but it doesn't have the snap it once did. Well, if I had but one son—"

Susan stepped beside her father and laid a reassuring hand on his shoulder. "Don't be worrying. As long as your crew is faithful to you, all is well enough."

"I sometimes doubt that," Old Pierre muttered. "I have let Luke Only do too much hiring and firing. But if he or either of his chips disobey me this day I will kill them with my own hands! There must be no more war. Nothing is worth it. I have had bad dreams ever since. Well, a man grows older and less bitter. The land is big enough for us all." He glanced up to study his daughter. Straight and supple she stood, without the Champifer stoop, without the darkness of skin. She had the black eyes of the family, yet Old Pierre had never discovered in them the harbored thirst of retaliation so character-istic of the tribe. Her mother's blood had been far gen-tler, far better than his own. "I have tried to raise you as a son," said Old Pierre. "The ranch is some day yours. And then what? By Godfrey, I'd like to be surer of Luke Only and Nuck. Little William can be led. Of him I have no great worry. But the others—" He got up. "If they betray me today I will kill them!"

"Who is to be their sheriff this term?" Susan asked.

"Lone Star's oldest son—Allan."

"Oh, Allan," the girl murmured. She was looking through the door. "I have seen them across the way, but he isn't in town yet."

Old Pierre's attention snapped to her face and remained there a long, studious minute. The girl didn't meet his eyes, but she felt the force of them, whether of pleasure or displeasure she could not tell. Her father had queer contradictions to his nature; he had fought the Boadleys, yet never had she heard him say an unkind word of any one of them.

"Let's eat," said Old Pierre, and led the way to the dining room.

Outside, and somewhat removed from the hotel, Luke Only held a short conference with his two sons. "What you arguing against Pierre for?" he demanded of Nuck. "That don't get you nowhere. Like busting your fist anunst a stone wall."

"Well, I'm sick of this dummy business," Nuck growled. "I'll be no dummy for Allan Boadley. If I run for Sheriff I want to be sheriff, see. Uncle is getting a mite soft-hearted. Nothing good ever come from that side of the river. Nothing will. They can be fought and they can be licked."

Luck Only's face was screwed in a knot. A shrewd, malicious smile penetrated the metal stubble. "They ain't got so many men as they used to have," he murmured. "My guess is, they ain't anxious to fight."

"They been running us long enough," Nuck persisted, growing more and more angry. "Champifers was in the country first. It had ought to be all Champifer range. Anyhow, I ain't going to be a dummy."

Little William said nothing. He seldom said anything. But whatever his father or older brother decided upon he would willingly agree to do. That was the essence of Little William. And it took no son of a seer to see that the two older ones were nosing the wind, hitching the gun-belts a little higher. Luke Only grinned. "Well, Nuck, you back me up when the showdown comes. I'll rig it."

"Now you're talking proper," Nuck said. "War is all right with me. It won't take much to whip them down. I want to see our brand all the way east of White River."

"And yourself owning it?" Luke Only prompted.

"Why not?" Nuck countered. "Right now we're only working for Pierre and Susan. We ain't got a stitch of property."

"Ambition is a Champifer habit," Luke Only agreed, and thereupon walked off, his eyes tallying certain members of the Champifer crew. Some were directly in his path, yet he avoided them. Others he had to seek out. To the first of these he beckoned.

"Old Pierre wants you should vote for Allan Boadley. Them's orders."

The puncher inclined his head. "All right."

But Luke Only repeated the statement a second time,

placing undue stress on the "want." His eyelids fluttered; the puncher grinned and turned on his heel. And for the next half hour Luke Only repeated this little performance to some twenty-odd Champifer riders. Then, considering his work done, he repaired to the restaurant and ate a substantial meal.

Grail City broiled under the down-slanting rays of the sun. The tide of life receded from the exposed street, restaurant dishes clattered, and in the spacious shade of the stables men squatted, drawing aimless figures in the dirt, swapping yarns. And it was during this midday lull that a lone traveler eased himself into the confines of the town from the Boadley side, stabled a jaded horse and proceeded on foot toward the hotel. His was a figure to inspire no poems, being excessively short and skinny. He walked on the outer edge of his feet with a peculiar side-winding motion and ample daylight passed between a pair of legs as crooked as ice-tongs. Beneath a Stetson that shaded him like a parasol was a weak chin, a button of a mouth decently draped by a mustache, and eyes that seemed touched by an Arctic frost. Notwithstanding these handicaps he proceeded in staid dignity to the hotel, took up a pen and wrote his name upon the register in a fair flowing hand—T. Ulysses Gove.

The clerk studied the name at length. In this land men seldom owned a middle name and practically never wrote it in the end-for-end fashion the stranger had used. That sort of thing smacked of the effete East. The clerk, being somewhat of a wag, was about to make a

16

suitable comment when he raised his face and looked directly into the eyes of T. Ulysses Gove. Thereupon the happy jest died aborning.

"Any comments?" suggested T. Ulysses Gove.

"None at all," was the clerk's hasty reply.

"You're a man of discretion," said T. Ulysses Gove, and went into the dining room. The noon-day rush was over. A pair of languid waitresses struggled with the wreckage while T. Ulysses Gove found himself a clear space adjacent to a gentleman obviously from the outside world and obviously a salesman. The salesman measured T. Ulysses Gove with a bold glance, reached for a toothpick, and heartily announced himself. "Name's Altgeld. Hardware's my line. Interested in hardware?"

T. Ulysses Gove was prospecting various platters and bowls. "None but what I carry on my person," he replied. "And I would advise you to do the same."

The salesman left. T. Ulysses Gove salvaged a lone T-bone, judiciously applied the ketchup and ate. Being a man of simple tastes he consumed no great amount of time in the gustatory proceedings and presently was back on the porch, piecing out his appetite with a chew of tobacco. He seemed a weary, disinterested figure and it appeared the brim of his Stetson was about to collapse and smother him. Nevertheless T. Ulysses Gove missed no movement on that river-split street. Men were knotting up over on the Champifer side. On the Boadley bank, silence held and punchers were moving deliberately out of sight. A pair of them rolled by T. Ulysses Gove and he caught the backwash of their talk.

"Who's running for us?"

"Allan."

"Well, he'll fight or he'll be peaceful. Fifty-fifty with that hombre. Where's he at?"

"Out in the Medicals as per usual. He knows that range better'n I know the toes on my feet. Me, I like flat country. He'd ought to be here. It's feeling kind of dubious in the air—"

They passed on. T. Ulysses Gove raised his head, projected a liquid parabola across the sidewalk and thought, No bird of peace ever abided in this county. It's the birthplace of original sin. Hell ain't far over the hump. Fifteen years it's been a-coming and it won't be long now. This town's going to be a slaughter pen. That water will run red. No wonder the buzzards like to live hereabouts.

It was exactly one o'clock by T. Ulysses Gove's two-pound watch when the procession of Champifers started across the bridge. At the van marched Old Pierre. Beside this chieftain strode the sullen Nuck and the smooth-faced Little William. Pair by pair the Champifer crew followed suit, the line lengthening until it stretched from the west bank to the polling place. They numbered more than fifty according to Gove's careful count, and though he was no great hand to indulge in imaginative flights there was a touch of prophecy to the onward rolling of the clan. Old Pierre and Nuck vanished inside the polling place. The line came to a halt, and thereupon the day swung along its second half as the tedious ceremony of voting was consummated. One after another the Champifer partisans emerged and went casually back to the west half of the town. T. Ulysses Gove's sharp eye saw them go into the saloon and he chalked another score in favor of the buzzards. A straight-limbed girl with a clear face stood across the way and watched the door of the polling place. Gove saw a line of worry on that face.

This ain't no situation for a lady, he reflected. She'd ought to be out of this brew of poison.

For the best part of two hours he saw her standing in the same spot, or until the last of the Champifer crew had cast a ballot and returned to safer territory. Upon that signal the Boadley side erupted men from all manner of places and converged toward the booth in Markowitz's store. The two punchers came back past Gove. This time they were not talking and it appeared to him that they carried themselves with an exaggerated carelessness. It was a plain sign—they were some worried. And T. Ulysses Gove found himself touched with a small excitement. Lone Star Boadley sat in his saddle and counted noses as his men arrived. Presently he was joined by other Boadleys—all golden-haired men, all tall and substantially built—and thus they were ranged in front of the store. T. Ulysses Gove waited while the shadows grew longer. He consumed the last of his plug. He eased himself on the porch for the twentieth time. He made rapid calculations in his little head.

"Half a hundred Champifers—less than twenty-five Boadleys," he mused aloud. "Them boys had ought to stay off the booze."

And then it was done. The last man had voted and reappeared in the street. A cold current seemed to sweep the town and touch every soul. The saloon on Champifer territory gave up its contents and there was an ominous note in the manner the members of that faction arrayed themselves beside the doorways, in convenient alleys, or at any niche that formed shelter. A pair of them, Gove saw, were framed in the second-story window of a building. Some of the Boadley crew likewise began to spread out, only to be checked by Lone Star's peremptory command, "Stay put." The girl across the way had disappeared. The traveling salesman came out of the hotel and stood beside Gove, nervously plucking at his vest buttons.

"What's all this about—what's it about, friend?"

"You'd better go back and polish some of your hardware," said T. Ulysses Gove. He bent forward. Somebody shot out of the polling place, flinging up an arm. A single phrase carried down the street and across the river, its import rolling along like a tidal wave.

"Champifer elected! Champifer elected by a full twenty-three votes!"

The Boadley crew accepted it as a challenge. The group wavered and all of a sudden broke into a dozen flying fragments. Men streamed by T. Ulysses Gove. Luke Only ducked from the polling place, his stubbled face wreathed in a shifty grin, and walked swiftly

20

across the bridge to his own territory. High up rose a shrill yell—as thin as the top note on a clarinet.

"There never was a Champifer honest enough to live with a thief!"

An answer came slapping back across the strip of water: "It ain't the place of yellow dogs to pass judgment! None of you rats could get a job on a decent outfit!"

"Yeah? Well we get our beef by natural methods, boy, and we don't carry no running irons under the saddle skirts either!"

"You'll eat them words before sunrise, brother!"

"Mebbe—but we don't eat mutton!"

Lone Star Boadley's yellow head waved above the crowd. His horse circled and galloped toward the bridge. Old Pierre Champifer came striding to meet him, afoot. And as the two came together the parrying of hot words and the rapid exchange of insults died to a murmur. The peace of Grail County trembled on the scales, to be swayed, kept or broken by the slightest nod from either chief. Old Pierre's face was a battle-ground of emotion; across it passed wave upon wave of rage. He jerked his head backward, summoning Nuck and Luke Only as a man might call a pair of dogs. Lone Star Boadley said nothing at all until Old Pierre had straightened before him; then a soft phrase escaped him.

"We're both sitting on a crater, Champifer. I'll let you take care of this your own way."

Old Pierre's cheek muscles stood out across his face.

"My friend, this truce will be kept. You two—come up here!"

Nuck and Luke Only advanced side by side. Old Pierre swung half around to command them. His finger stabbed at Luke Only, and such was the impact of his hard eyes that Luke Only's sly grin evaporated. "What have you done?" Old Pierre demanded. "I told you to choose twenty-five men to vote for Allan Boadley. That was my order. What have you done?"

"Well, I told them," Luke Only grumbled. "But if they don't want to vote for a Boadley, it can't be helped."

"You lie!" said Old Pierre. "You have played to make this surly son of yours a sheriff at my expense. Well, sir, you'll undo that piece of work now. I run the Champifers, understand it?"

"What's done is done," Luke Only grunted, and turned to Nuck for help.

"Guess I'm duly constituted sheriff," Nuck agreed. "That's all. It's no more than right, is it? We're a majority. You can tell the Boadleys I'll treat them as square as they'd treat us."

Old Pierre stepped forward a foot. Both his hands came up and struck Nuck flat on the face, one cheek and then the other. The report of these two blows carried out from the bridge and down to where T. Ulysses Gove sat. Nuck jerked away, his dark face draining of color. "I'll not stand that from anybody!" he shouted. "Keep your dirty hands off me!"

But Old Pierre's anger had hardened. Lone Star

Boadley, a silent witness, saw in the man a flooding up of that controlled vindictiveness which fifteen years before had made him a terror on the range. "You will resign in favor of Allan Boadley," said Old Pierre in a dead level voice. "Say it in just so many words."

"I'll resign for no Boadley!" cried Nuck. "I'm rightfully elected!"

"You will resign," Old Pierre repeated, "or I'll drop you in your tracks."

"That's going too strong," Luke Only interrupted. "It's your own flesh, Pierre."

"I have killed before. I will do it again if you try to betray me."

"Wait a minute," said Lone Star Boadley. "It won't help for him to resign. That don't make Allan a sheriff."

"Then we will hold another election on the spot," Old Pierre decided.

"I'm afraid to trust my men with yours," Lone Star objected. "But here's a suggestion. Have Nuck appoint Allan a deputy. Then have Nuck resign. Allan will then be legally an officer."

"It is done," Old Pierre answered, and again bent the threat of his glance on Nuck. "Now, my fine conspirator, go through with this little ceremony."

The sun had fallen across the western rim, leaving Grail City in a purple twilight. Almost immediately these four men on the bridge were shadowed. Nuck looked over his shoulder to all the Champifer crew lined along the street. It appeared he was about to call on them. Old Pierre moved slightly. There was the click

23

of a lock, and when Nuck's attention returned it was to face the muzzle of a gun. "Go on," Old Pierre directed. "You are no more to me than a stray animal."

Nuck threw back his head. "All right. I'm appointing Allan Boadley—damn his yellow belly—deputy sheriff. I resign. Let it go. But here and now I serve warnin' on you—you'll regret this to your dying day! That applies to all Boadleys as well!"

Somewhere he had got the sheriff's badge of authority. It glinted a moment in his hand, and then he flung it far from him. It fell with a sheering splash into the river. In no plainer way could he have told the multitude of his surrender of authority. He turned so quickly that he struck Luke Only a sharp blow, and strode off the bridge. Old Pierre faced Lone Star Boadley and inclined his head, once more grave and self-contained. "The reins are in your hands. I will remind you of the agreement again. In the course of your son's duties he will at no time cross into our territory. If there is something to be done or someone to be apprehended west of the river, he will notify me."

"Agreed," said Lone Star. "I will bid you good day."

The scene was over. Lone Star rode back to his assembled sons, dismounted, and strode thoughtfully toward the hotel. Lights sprang up in the town and a banjo began plunking out its tantalizing chords. The saloons were reaping harvest. T. Ulysses Gove smoked cigarettes in the shadows. "Postponed," he decided. "But not for long. The stars are plumb set to collide. God made man to suffer and die. This county is due for another purge and a lot of boys will sleep in the dust."

Within the hotel lobby Lone Star Boadley confronted his sons. He had four, and three of them were with him now: Snass, Robe and Strickland, in the order of their age, all with golden yellow hair, all tall and stalwart men with the Boadley phlegm about them. And as Lone Star's blue eyes ranged from one to the other he seemed to settle into a kind of moodiness. He seemed to look through and beyond them, reading something of the future.

"We come near to war," said he. "May the Lord avert such a thing. One was plenty. But it takes fire to burn a man and there's too many young hot-heads over yonder who pine for action. It looks to me as if Old Pierre ain't got the control over his camp he used to have. We'll have to walk soft and hope for the best."

The hotel door swung back, slamming against the inner wall. In swung a tall and rangy man with a sombrero set to an angle and a bronzed face that swept all things at a humorous glance. He was a Boadley—the roughly chiseled features and the yellow hair indicated that—but he possessed a quality the rest of the Boadleys lacked: a restless humor, a buoyancy that bubbled up and spilled out, a sense of fraternity that unconsciously drew men's attention and interest. As he came nearer the group it was to be seen that he stood an inch above the tallest and that he lacked little of the family bulk. He walked with springy muscles; he carried himself with the lazy indolence of one sure of the power in reserve behind that indolence. A dozen feet removed from them he stopped, tilted back his Stetson and included them all at one graceful sweep of his arm.

"My presence ain't required in this august assemblage, but the beans ran out and the lure of gold grew dreary. Esteemed brothers, reverend sir, what sad fact dims the luster of your orbs?"

Lone Star smiled, a rare smile for him. "You're now deputy sheriff, Allan."

"The hell I am," Allan said, losing his grin. "Another one of those comic opera elections? Who's sheriff?"

"Nuck Champifer was. He appointed you—and resigned."

Being versed in the rules of the county, Allan didn't miss the implication. He meditated upon it over a brown paper cigarette, blew a ceremonial ring toward the ceiling and shook his yellow head. "I smelled trouble thirty miles up in the Medicals. That's why I came. It may be the water, it may be the air, or it may be the natural born perversity of man—but I'm damned if I see why Grail County has to be an armed camp. Me duputy? Say, that's sad."

Lone Star shook his head. "You're the law enforcer for two years. Just you sit down somewhere and study it out, my boy. It'll take all you got to keep things smooth and that's why I stood you up for the job. I'm going down to the corrals. Be back in a minute. Round up the boys, Snass. We're riding out before somebody starts shooting."

He left the hotel. Allan shrugged and followed after.

His father had vanished somewhere in the shadows, so Allan wandered down the street, idly noting the sights. Already he had begun to feel the weight of his job. It was a two-year sentence, nothing less; and for just that length of time he couldn't call himself a free man. No more roaming up in the pine crested Medicals, no more dawdling over a camp fire.

To hell with such a job, he grumbled.

Across the way the Champifers were gathering, evidently for the out trail. Allan came abreast the door of Markowitz's store and was about to pass on when a woman's voice reached him.

"—dotted Swiss curtaining, Mr. Markowitz. They haven't got it across the way."

Allan threw up an arm. The girl stepped unexpectedly through the doorway and struck him fairly. It was Susan Champifer with a little packet of goods under one arm. Allan stepped aside, reaching for his Stetson. "I'm like the town pump," he said humbly. "Always in the road."

She rested just an instant against the doorsill, her body relaxed, looking up into his bronzed face, never smiling, never saying a word. The color came to her cheeks and some emotion passed below the surface of her eyes. Then she straightened and seemed literally to fly across the beam of light emanating from the store and on into the darkness. Allan thought he heard her saying, "I'm sorry, Allan Boadley," but he wasn't any too sure of it. Later, he heard her light feet drumming across the bridge. Markowitz called to him.

"Mister Allan, come a minute here. Something I got to tell—"

The smash of a gunshot shook the town, the echo racing down the street, snapping at every frayed nerve. Men stopped dead in their tracks and of a sudden all activity ceased. T. Ulysses Gove rose from his seat on the hotel porch and spat out his chew. "It's come," he said solemnly. "There ain't a man, beast or bird safe in Grail County from now on."

2.   The cast boot heel

The echo of that shot had scarcely died before Allan was away from the store and going on into the shadows whence the sound had come. Boadley partisans were spilling from the saloon, clustering up into knots. Some ran toward the bridge, some struck after Allan. A lantern waved in the darkness like a firefly. Men shouted from spot to spot and within sixty seconds there was a loosely flung line of them from one end of the street to the other. Snass and Robe and Strickland Boadley came swinging out of the hotel, shoulder to shoulder, challenging whoever crossed their path. Over on the west side, the Champifers were a-saddle, the long line of horsemen moving slowly into the night. Allan, looking across the water at this parade of strength, saw Nuck Champifer spurring posthaste up from the rear of the column toward the front. The sullen one held his sombrero in one fist and used it like a quirt while the black hair streamed down over his

28

eyes. Haste rode at his back; he appeared to be drunk.

The shot seemed to have occurred on the north end of the town, past the livery stable and in the neighborhood of the corrals. That way Allan took his search, more greatly concerned than the occasion justified. For it was no uncommon event to have a puncher set forth upon the street and vent his state of mind with a six-gun puncturing the sky. What troubled him was the knowledge that upon this night anything might happen. The farther he went, the slower he walked, eyes sweeping the opaque pall that screened the town. The moon was a thin crescent, the stars dim. To his left he heard the sluggish waters of the diminutive river lapping against the bank. Something moved ahead and he spoke sharply. *"Quien es?"* There was no answer. Another lantern bobbed down the long alley of the stable, borne by the roustabout. Allan, a dozen yards beyond the stable and directly by the river bank, stumbled against a yielding substance. Someone lying there—and before he dropped and ran an exploring arm along the body he knew the man to be dead. He summoned the roustabout. "Bring that lantern here!"

The roustabout came on the run. The lantern's rays touched the prone figure, lying face upward, sightless eyes staring at the black canopy of the sky. Allan rose and turned his back. That man was his father—Lone Star Boadley, the builder of the Boadley Empire—and even in the sudden overwhelming upheaval of spirit, young Allan's mind raced far ahead of the tragedy, to foresee a still greater one. His own men were advancing. The Champifer crew had not yet quite got clear of the town. Another minute and there would be a flaming of guns. Allan seized the lantern and turned down the wick. The roustabout said nothing at all, for he had seen how utterly cold and bleak this Boadley's eyes had become.

"Keep your mouth shut for twenty minute," Allan said. "Not a word out of you. Go fetch my brothers!"

"By God, Allan, ain't there no killing in you?" the roustabout protested.

"Enough to kill you, if you open your loose face. Get along!"

The first of the punchers stumbled onward, demanding information. "What's up over there?"

"Nothing to get excited about," Allan said. "Better get your liquor down. We're leaving in a minute."

The roustabout started away, mumbling to himself. But he didn't get far. The rest of the Boadleys were already upon him, carrying another lantern. And behind them trooped a solid group of punchers. Thus had the invisible telegraph warned them; or rather, that strange sense of danger that moved in each man of the range. This shot had been like a thousand other shots, yet it had emptied the saloon and drawn them along irresistibly. Snass's voice carried up. "What's up?"

Allan answered quickly. "Get the men together, Snass. We're riding out."

"What's up?" Snass persisted.

"Never mind, never mind. Do as I tell you. Get the crew in the saddle. Robe and Strick there? Come here."

"Orders," said Snass. "Get your horses, boys. No palavering there. It's the new sheriff speaking words. On the prod."

The crew halted, turned about and moved toward the hitching racks. Allan waited until the last straggler was beyond earshot. Robe and Strick were beside him, silent after their habitual manner. Allan muttered something that made no sense and turned up the lantern wick. He still had his back to his father; nor would he look at his brothers. He wanted never to see their faces. So he waited while the stars seemed to grow even smaller and more remote and the faint night wind rippled against the branches of a nearby cottonwood. Robe was speaking in a faraway voice. "Where's his gun?"

"In his fist," Strickland whispered. "Doubled under his chest. Don't you see? I bet all the cartridges is there. Allan, damn your soul, turn out that light! No—wait."

"Stick in your tracks," Allan muttered. "I want to look at this ground." He moved quite slowly around Lone Star, sweeping the lantern back and forth. Robe had dropped to his knees and now made a discovery. "Right in the heart. The gent was close. Old man would be facing the way he fell, wouldn't he? Well, then, the bullet came from the corrals, and whoever pulled the trigger wasn't more than five yards off. Had to be that close to hit the mark."

"Old man turned over before he died," Allan said. "No bullet would knock him backward. He'd fall face forward. Which makes the bullet come from the river."

31

He completed his circle and stood half down the bank of the river, eyes close to the sandy five-foot shelving. Snass was returning, impatient at the delay, throwing his questions through the shadows. Robe spoke softly, so softly that Allan didn't hear the words. And then Snass fell silent. The lantern bobbed up over the bank again, revealing Allan's expressionless face. "Tracks dug deep. Fella made a running jump, forded the river and got over to Champifer side. But he left a little souvenir—Snass, you're the gods' most awful fool!"

But Snass was the oldest and he had known his father best. Therefore his face was wet and wrinkled. "What was all the delay about?"

"Wanted the Champifers to get out before the crew discovered what'd happened. There'd have been war on the spot. Well, they're all gone now. Snass, you get a buckboard. Have some of the boys do it. Come on to the hotel. This has got to be ironed out."

"Go ahead," Snass said. "I'll take care of this. Well, the light went out. Hell, I had lots of things I'd like to've told the old gent. And the light went out—"

"Come away from here," Allan murmured to the others. Down the street they walked, past the gathered punchers and on into the hotel. Allan wasted no time coming to the point. He extended his fist and opened it; therein rested a boot heel such as was worn on all footgear in cattle land—a long and tapering piece of wood that securely held a boot into the stirrup. "Fella knocked it loose when he jumped that bank," he said.

"Champifer doings," Strickland grunted; and being

the youngest the war spirit was the soonest to rise in him. "You did wrong to let that gang get away, Allan. They've got to be smashed."

"Easy," Allan cautioned. "We don't know who wore this. It's just a starting point. I've got to find out."

"What next?" asked Robe. Of all the Boadleys he was the most imperturbable. His voice seldom rose above a medium pitch and he had never been seen excited. Perhaps he was the only man in Grail County who neither smoked nor chewed, but he was perpetually wadding up a stick of gum and flicking it to the back of his tongue. That constituted a true index to his temper—the more gum he chewed the nearer he was to the boiling point. "Going to follow those tracks acrost the river, Allan?"

"I can't," said Allan. "It's the agreement. No Champifer sheriff ever stepped into our territory and we've got to do likewise. But there's one little thing I can do." He scanned the empty lobby, lowering his voice. "I can see a certain party across the river."

Snass came through the door, grim and foreboding. "Boys, running the ranch is a four-way proposition from now on. We'd better decide who's to be Number One. Somebody's got to do the figuring, sign the checks and keep the fences up."

"No doubt about that," Allan said. "You're Number One. Let Robe and Strick split the riding boss job between them."

"What about you?" Snass countered.

"I got a job," Allan said, and the other three knew

33

what he meant without asking. "But you fellows know I never did care much for this rigged-up election stuff. I'd as soon let the Champifers take the job for keeps. They can't injure us and they'd be pretty bold to run any rannies. Anyhow, things stand plumb uncertain at present. There ain't any sheriff and I doubt my legal status as deputy. There's got to be another election. Right away. When you go to Judge Addis's ranch, Snass, stop in and have him call a special vote. I'll stay on the job till then. Nothing but trouble can come of me being sheriff and at the same time trying to run down the gent that got the old man."

"You're the doctor," Snass agreed. "By the way, I'm sending Jeff Harlow down to ride line along the Sinks. River's dry there. Cattle might cross over to Champifer range. Let's go, boys. You staying in town, Allan?"

"Yep."

Snass started for the door. "I'll leave three-four of the crew in town then. You may need them for chores. As for me, I can guess where that bullet came from, but I'll bide my time till you find out the particular hombre that pulled the trigger. Then, whatever may come of it, we're going to get him if we got to shoot every last—"

"Soft on names, Snass," Allan warned. "I share those sentiments. But we'll move careful. We're on the ragged edge of a range war this minute."

"I'll do nothing to aggravate one—and mighty little to stop one," Snass said, and led his brothers out to the street. Allan paused on the porch and watched the Boadley outfit ride by. Directly behind his brothers came a flat-bed wagon. Lone Star was taking his last ride across Grail County, a blanket covering him. Allan raised his hat and stumbled away.

He had, at the moment, no sense of direction. But, somewhere in the shadows of the sidewalk, he felt a hand touch him. It was Markowitz, the store man. "A letter I should give to you," Markowitz said. He pressed it into Allan's fist. "Don't ask who wrote. I ain't to tell."

Allan got hold of himself and looked around. "All right, Markowitz. Listen, will you do a favor for me? Circle down to the lower end of town and cross the river by the shallows. Don't let anybody see you. Fetch Shoe Jim to the back of your store."

Markowitz vanished. Allan went on into the store and opened his letter. It was unsigned and the clear, back-slanting lines bore a warning:

"Allan Boadley: I have no particular reason to be a friend of yours. I am NOT a friend of yours. But I can't stand by and see any man shot down. You are in danger. Never let yourself be careless. You have a reputation for not guarding your back, not caring who stands behind you. And there is some one who means to take advantage of that fact."

A woman's writing. Allan recalled the queer, intent glance Susan Champifer had bent upon him as she stood resting against the door sill. Why should she care enough about his safety to thus put him on guard? He passed behind a counter and let himself through a rear door that brought him to Markowitz's store room. A solitary lantern hung on the wall. He waited five long minutes. Markowitz came back; he heard the store-keeper moving in the front of the place, engaged in a solitary monologue. "By Omaha, why should I buy such cheap goods what cost me so much? I am a robber to charge such prices and still I cheat myself. If it gets worse I go to New York and push a cart once more." Knuckles drummed on the rear door. The door opened, and Shoe Jim squeezed himself through and twisted away from the opening.

Shoe Jim was the county's nearest approach to a secret agent. Though he had his shoe shop on the Champifer side and outwardly subscribed to the Champifer code, he had for many years served Lone Star with valuable information. Shoe Jim's career fol-lowed the customary Western arc: once he rode the range, but when his riding days were over he settled in town, took the trade he knew something about and grew fat. His roly-poly head was thatched with short white hair that looked like moss on a tree. He could make anybody laugh at his philosophies and he seemed perpetually to be beaming. But close observation might reveal that these fine lines of humor splaying out from his eyes came from undue flesh and had nothing to do with his disposition. Shoe Jim was shrewd. He had a doubtful set of ethics and he loved intrigue. "What's up, Allan?"

Allan brought the boot heel from his pocket. "Ever

see this in your shop, Jim?"

Shoe Jim took the heel and tested it with a professional eye. "Lots of 'em like it, Allan. This come with the boot. It wasn't put on by me."

"All right," Allan said. "But somebody's riding the range minus one heel. The fellow may know it, or he maybe hasn't discovered it yet. But I'm betting he'll bring that boot to you for fixing. When he does, let me know. On the quiet, Jim."

Shoe Jim winked, which was a ponderous dropping of both lids. "Depend on me. And while we're on the subject, I want you to know, anything I can do, why just lemme know. They're a powerful lot of war talk on my side of the river. More'n I've heard in nine year. It's the young bloods. Afraid it won't blow over, either, this time. Too much fire behind the smoke."

"Well, we'll have to do the best we can. I'll turn down the lantern."

In the semi-darkness, Shoe Jim opened the door and let himself out. Allan went forward and into the street. T. Ulysses Gove stood near at hand, seeming to see nothing. Allan paused to light a cigarette, at which Gove, looking in the opposite direction, spoke up. "Like to see you a minute, Boadley. I'll be up in room three of the hotel."

He moved away. Allan waited until the small figure with the ridiculously big hat appeared in the light of the hotel door. Then he followed, went into the lobby and on upstairs to the designated room. T. Gove stood in the middle of the floor.

37

"You did right," Gove said mildly. "Plumb dead right about holding off your men till the Champifers got away. Takes a level head to think through like that. But it's only a temporary peace, friend. A damn temporary one." He flipped back the lapel of his coat to reveal a star hooked high on his shirt. "T. Ulysses Gove is the name. Sheriff of Snake County."

"Pleased to know you," Allan acknowledged, extending his hand. Gove took it and limply waggled his fingers.

"I hold here," Gove explained, ferreting around his inner pocket, "a warrant which I'd like you to execute. Man of your county wanted over our way for murder. Indicted by last grand jury. Case is two years old but we just got wind of some clues."

"Who's the man?"

Gove's cold eyes met Allan's. The small one seemed actually to grow wary. "Name's Nuck Champifer."

Allan shook his head slowly. He accepted the warrant, read it line for line. "Do you know Nuck by sight?" he asked.

"Seen him this afternoon," admitted T. Ulysses Gove.

"Why didn't you serve this on me while he was in town?"

Gove manufactured himself a brown paper cigarette, sealed it with the tip of his tongue, crimped the ends and applied a match with meticulous care. The match he pinched out, broke it in twain and deposited both fragments in a vest pocket. After three sparing puffs he crumbled the cigarette and thrust it into the same receptacle with the broken match. One skinny hand whipped a plug of tobacco out of some rear aperture in his loose clothes. "Didn't want to bust in on your affairs at that particular moment," he said. "'Twas too ticklish. What if I had told you? We couldn't a-got him then."

"We might have tried."

"Trying ain't doing," was Gove's sagacious answer. "All we'd got for our troubles would a-been some hot lead. It wasn't nowise the proper time. I take it you're new at this sheriff business? Well, man and boy, I been camping on the job some twenty years. Been in some tough rows, too. Ain't got creased yet. Why? Because I never tried to catch a crook in one day when I had two days to spare. If it looked like a week's trailing I always made double the time. If a gent looked like he was heading acrost a state line I usually let him go because I knew he wouldn't come back. Saves expenses of a trial, as well as grub in jail. Never tried to get the drop on a man unless I knew I could pull the gun faster. If I couldn't I caught him some other way. Conservation has always been my motto."

Allan smiled. "Food for thought in that statement, Gove."

"I wouldn't be gassing so much," the small one apologized, "only I figured the experience of an old hand might help. Seen too many young deputies try to match slugs with a crook, thinking it the only dignified course to follow. Sounds neat but it's sure hard on deputies. Best to catch a skunk with a long pole."

"I'll keep the warrant," Allan said. "Are you waiting here or going back?"

"Got plenty of time," T. Ulysses Gove explained. "Expenses being all paid and the grub here is better'n I get home. How you figure to broach this matter?"

"Send for Old Pierre Champifer. He runs that family."

"I knowed you had a good head," Gove approved. "Another thing, don't recognize me on the street for the time being. No use me being prematurely involved."

Allan went out of the room and back to the street. Twenty minutes later, he had raised an idle puncher on the Champifer side and dispatched him off to Old Pierre with a summons to Grail City.

That's some more fuel on the fire, he thought, sitting on the hotel porch. God only knows where this will end. Wistfully, he pictured the cool pine forest up in the Medicals and of the solitary night camps he had made there. A coyote's cry trembled out along the desert.

3. The red horseman rides

The Champifers reached their home ranch unaware of the murder in Grail City. And as was the custom after pilgrimages to town, Susan made a pot of coffee for her father and settled beside the fireplace, watching the light play upon his dark cheeks. He had won another fight with Luke Only and Nuck, yet it seemed to her that victory sat heavy on his shoulders. Something oppressed him. From time to time he raised his head

40

and studied the girl, and after such an inspection his eyes passed over her to where Nuck moodily sat. These late months had seen a softening of Old Pierre as well as an increasing taciturnity. He was troubled of spirit tonight.

"Nuck, my boy," said he, "if I treated you harshly, it was of your own making."

Nuck refused to answer. His lips were drawn a little back from his teeth in the manner of one rehearsing unpleasant memories and he stared sulkily at the floor. Luke Only, draped at a far corner, smiled grimly. Father and son were of the same stubborn piece of clay, animated by the same unforgiving spirit. Old Pierre spoke more rapidly.

"Let it be a lesson. I rule this outfit. I've given you plenty of room to exercise your own will—that applies as well to you, Luke—but it seems I've let you run too loose. You know my inclination as regards the Boadleys. We'll be at peace with them."

"That's what you say," Nuck muttered.

"Yes, it's what I say, you rat!" cried Old Pierre, roused again. "And you'll obey it or I'll hunt you like a coyote!"

Nuck sprang up from his chair, shaking with rage. "For the last time, keep your tongue off me. I gave in to you and them damned Boadleys, but don't figure I'm forgetting. You'll live to regret it to the last breath you take—and so will them yellow-haired oxen! Mebbe you think you run this ranch. Come right down to cases, I ain't sure you do!"

41

Luke Only warned his son. "Easy on that, Nuck. Easy."

Nuck turned on his father. "What you holding back for? It's your quarrel, too. Why should I pull all the chestnuts out of the fire? I'll sting somebody for this, you'd better believe! I ain't recognizing no Boadley as sheriff. I ain't recognizing nobody's right to tell me what I should do! From now on I play my own hand!"

"Not on this ranch," Old Pierre snapped.

"Then I'll pull out!" shouted Nuck. "And listen—you won't live forever. After you're gone do you think us folks is going to herd stock at Susan's orders? Not by a—"

Luke Only came out of his corner quickly. "Shut your mouth, Nuck! Shut it, I say!"

"So that's what you pair have been cooking up, eh?" Old Pierre lowered his coffee cup. His narrow face became both harsh and cruel, with a cruelty he had struggled all his mature life to bridle. "I'll attend to that. From now on neither of you leave this ranch without my express permission. If you do I'll send a posse to bring you back and I'll put a whip on your bare shoulders with my own hand. I'll tie you to the snubbing post, strip-naked in the sun." At a single stride he was out of his chair and standing over Nuck. Susan averted her face, not wishing to see the latent murder in her father's eyes. But she understood now, for the first time, why men were so scrupulously courteous to him, and how he himself walked in fear of his temper. "That is what I will do to you," he told Nuck. "And I have never gone back on my word yet, you black-hearted rascal!"

"Come away," Luke Only muttered. He forced Nuck to turn and shoved him out of the door. Old Pierre stood in his tracks until the sound of their boots had dragged across the porch and were lost in the yard. Then he went back to his chair and sat down as one supremely tired. He took up the coffee cup and drained the last cold dregs, the cup shaking.

"I'm losing my grip," he growled. "Best if they were dead. Twenty years ago I could have put them out of the way and never minded."

"Dad—never say that again!"

There was the swift rush of a horse outside and the echo of other boots running across the porch. A man stood in the doorway with a slip of paper in his fist. "Come from Grail City, Mister Champifer," he said. "Allan Boadley would like to see you there right away. Here's a note."

Nuck appeared, watching Old Pierre intently as the latter unfolded and read the note; and the sullen one seemed to draw back and crouch a little when Old Pierre finished.

"Lone Star's dead," Old Pierre said solemnly. "And though he was a Boadley I admired the man." He stared at Nuck until the latter moved impatiently. "Saddle me a horse. I'm going in."

"What's Allan Boadley want?" Nuck demanded. "What does he say?"

"Saddle that horse," Old Pierre repeated. "As for

you—" indicating the messenger—"put up in the bunkhouse overnight." He tucked the note in his pocket, dropped his hand on his daughter's shoulder and went out. "Sands run fast when the bottle's near empty," he whispered to himself.

Nuck came up with a horse and repeated his question. Old Pierre only shook his head. A moment later he rode away. Nuck tarried until the Champifer chief was lost in the darkness; then he whirled about and ran for the corrals. Presently he, too, was riding toward Grail City. Susan, now in the doorway, caught a moment's sight of her cousin just before he left the yard.

Nuck kept his distance for three miles or better; but halfway into town he put a spur to his pony and presently saw Old Pierre outlined ahead of him in the dim starlight. Old Pierre had come to a halt, waiting. His challenge floated across the soft shadows. "Who's that?"

Nuck drew up. "What's Boadley want?"

"That is none of your business now," Old Pierre replied. "Go back to the house."

"What's he want?" Nuck persisted stubbornly. "Lemme see that writing."

"Get back to the house," Old Pierre said. "You have made enough trouble for one night."

Nuck fell silent. He seemed to be feeding on Old Pierre's last phrase. And of a sudden he crouched in his saddle, muttering, "I won't be took like that." His body swerved far over in his saddle. His right arm came up. There was a single explosion, and Old Pierre sighed,

44

relaxed and pitched to the ground. Nuck sprang out of his seat and ripped back Old Pierre's coat, searching every pocket. "I won't be took like that," he repeated aloud. Paper crackled in his hand as he ran around to his horse. And for the next few moments the man quite lost control of himself. A chill swept through him. He felt sick at his stomach. He started to jump into the saddle and changed his mind. He forgot about the paper still gripped in his fist. He turned aimlessly and, swayed by unreasoning instincts, struck into the desert at a dog trot. Fifty yards away, the cold air brought him to a stand.

Take it easy, he told himself. Nobody heard that shot. Godfrey, this has got to be covered up quick! Where's that note?

It was in his hand, as he presently discovered. He dropped to his haunches, lit a match and read it. Nothing there to incriminate him. Allan Boadley had merely announced the death of Lone Star and was asking Old Pierre to ride into town for talk. Nuck felt himself sag. He'd killed on a false suspicion, helped likewise by the burning anger rising out of the manner in which Old Pierre had treated him.

Still, that note meant something. A Boadley wouldn't be sending notes to a Champifer without cause. The old man would have caught on. He deserved to die . . . he wasn't no better than a Boadley, treating his own kin like so much scum . . .

The match went out. Nuck stared up to the sky. A long, long while he rested there, a figure alternately swayed by fear and anger and revenge. The more he considered the situation, the clearer it became he had an opportunity to wipe out the Boadleys root and branch. He found a stub of a pencil in his pocket and the back of an envelope. Lighting another match, he awkwardly wrote two sprawling lines:

"All Champifers take care. The peace is ended. This is some pay for killing Lone Star. And you'll pay more."

"Sounds reasonable," he muttered. He walked back to the dead Pierre and tucked the spurious warning in the old man's collar. Climbing into the saddle he made a wide sweep of the country and came to the home ranch by a back route. Nobody saw him arrive, nobody saw him put away his horse. Quietly he slipped into the house and went to bed.

It was near to supper of the following day. Allan Boadley sat in the sheriff's office at Grail City, reading the accumulated correspondence scattered through the desk drawers: reward notices for fugitives coming out of adjacent counties, circulars of the legislature appertaining to new range laws, and now and then some anonymous letter giving hints of rustling. All told, it made no imposing record. Grail County was unimportant in the state. Nothing happened to keep a sheriff riding or worrying; nothing but the ever-present feud between the two great factions. And so far this feud had been kept damped by skillful avoidance of the issue, the result of diplomacy on the part of Lone Star Boadley and Old Pierre Champifer.

Both of 'em diplomats, Allan mused. I guess my job is to be as good a smooth-oiled fellow as I can. It looks to me like that was an order I ain't going to fill. Clouds coming up. The day of peace is passing. Oh, well.

One of the townsmen stopped at the door. "They's a fella on the bridge wants to see you, Allan."

Allan left the office and walked across the street. A Champifer partisan had reined his horse in the exact center of the bridge. Allan noticed that the man carried his gun well forward, the holster flap tied back. A rifle was slung in a boot on one flank of the horse. The puncher waited somberly until Allan directly faced him. Then excitement glittered in his eyes.

"The Champifers told me to tell you they accepted the challenge," the puncher said.

"What challenge?" Allan asked.

The puncher wrinkled his nose and looked scornful. "The challenge pinned to Old Pierre's shirt collar, mister."

Allan peered at the man. "Where is Old Pierre?"

The puncher raised his shoulders. "In hell I'd reckon. Dead anyhow. That was a fine stunt—decoying him towards town with an invite and then plugging him. You Boadleys will burn for that."

The news of Old Pierre's death jolted Allan but he kept a poker face. "None of the Boadley outfit has crossed White River," he said finally.

47

The puncher grinned. "I'll tell that to the new bosses."

"Who are they?"

"Luke an' Nuck."

"Leaving the girl out of it, eh? She's the rightful heir, isn't she?"

"What's that got to do with you?" the puncher retorted. "I ain't here to answer questions. I give you the message. But if you want some advice I'd say you'd ought to streak acrost the Medicals as fast as the Lord give you strength. When you killed Old Pierre, you killed the only peaceable man in the outfit. We're fighting from now on."

Allan sighed. Then he said levelly, "You go back and tell Luke and Nuck that the Boadleys don't want to fight, haven't made any moves to start a fight. Tell them we kept on our own side. But if they have got to have trouble we won't run from it. And we didn't kill Old Pierre."

The puncher turned his horse and galloped off the bridge. Allan retreated to the sheriff's office and for a long hour stared at a blank wall. Old Pierre was dead. It seemed queer that both he and Lone Star should pass the same night—more than queer. Considering the friction between Old Pierre and the other three Champifer men it looked as if one of them had deliberately set out to remove all safeguards. Well, they chose a good time to wipe us off the map, he reflected. Wonder if that was the reason extra men were hired over there this season? Old Pierre didn't have a hand in it, but then he let Luke do most of the managing. As for us, we'll do well to muster twenty-five guns.

Unaccountably, his mind reverted to the girl as she had been revealed by the light from Markowitz's store—tall and free-limbed. Anger came to him. Why don't they keep their dirty paws off her? he thought. They'll beat her out of that ranch!

Dusk had come. Grail City was at the trenches again and the lone musician in the saloon twiddled a fandango from his guitar. Allan went to the street to find one of the Boadley crew left in town. Presently one of them ambled out of the restaurant.

"Hop aboard," Allan directed. "Go tell my brothers to keep a sharp lookout. Somebody dropped Old Pierre and the rest of that family have declared war."

"Judas!" the puncher breathed. "Merry hell coming down the road. How about you, Allan? They'll clean out this place first."

"My horse can travel as fast as any of theirs." Allan grinned. "But you bust the dust. Thunder rumbling over the west. I'm hoping the hot air will evaporate, but it's my feeling nothing will satisfy the Champifers now but total extinction of all Boadleys. I'm not so blamed sure they can't do it, either."

The puncher wheeled like a shot and vanished into the closing shadows. The tattoo of his horse's flying hoofs brought Grail City out of doors, and the guitar ceased its wheedling tune. Allan saw T. Ulysses Gove strolling past, and in the glow of the office light that gentleman's pinched countenance was bright and sharp. Presently Allan was aware of others casually marching past him and it seemed they looked his way with more than accustomed interest. Voices murmured down by the stables, cigarette tips traced across the night's smudge. Those men who had traveled past on foot came back a-saddle, dropped in front of the saloon's hitching rack and left their animals there. Grail City had hitched its belt tighter, that was quite apparent. Men were restless. They dropped into the saloon and out again. They moved along the street in pairs. They stopped in the deep shadows to watch the Champifer territory beyond the river. Somebody struggled with a second-story window, swearing in soft, honeyed syllables. The hardware store did good business.

Allan returned to the office. A fist struck twice on the back door and when he went over and opened it he found Markowitz crouching against the wall. "By Shoe Jim I should tell you a man came in with a boot to be fixed," Markowitz whispered. "A heel it was off. He is still there."

"Check," said Allan. Markowitz disappeared. Allan crossed to the street and stood a long interval staring at the river. For fifteen years both factions had observed the agreement to keep their own boundaries. He hated to break the rule; it meant that all hope of peace was gone. But Lone Star and Old Pierre were dead, a challenge had been laid down, and Lone Star's murderer was just across the way. Allan walked toward the stable and threw his saddle on a horse. He left the stable by the rear alley and cut around the back lots, coming to the river a quarter mile south of the town.

Shoe Jim will take his time putting on that heel, Allan thought, fording the stream. He struck a road, followed it a few yards and then marched out into the prairie and left his horse. The Champifer side of Grail City was next to deserted; hardly a sound rose from its row of scarred shacks. Something ominous in that silence. Like that vacuum in the atmosphere just preceding a storm. Allan reached the rear of Shoe Jim's place and laid his ear to the door. He heard Shoe Jim talking through a mouth full of tacks, talking slowly. It went on and on until the second party seemed to grow weary of palaver and broke in. A chair scraped. Allan deserted his post and crawled to an alleyway down which he commanded a view of the street. A tall body slid past the opening and vanished. Allan went back to the door, listened a moment and tapped lightly. Presently it opened a short inch. "Who's there?"

"Allan."

"It ain't that fella's boot, Allan. His foot is too big for it. He's doin' a chore for somebody else. Wasn't saying who, either."

"Who was the gent?"

"Cal Levering. Champifer brand."

"Thanks, Jim."

Allan retreated to his horse and rode swiftly into Champifer soil, angling somewhat to the north. The trail to the Champifer ranch ran over a flat stretch and dipped across an ancient branch of the river, long since dry. Allan came to this arroyo and halted in its depression, not twenty yards from the trail.

How far can I track this gent? he wondered. Will it carry me all the way to the ranch? Can't go that far. If the fellow who owns that boot ain't out here waiting then I'm up a stump. A thousand boots like that one, none of them branded.

The ground carried up the rhythmic progression of a horse on the trot. A moving outline passed the rim of the arroyo, dipped down and up and was gone. Allan edged to the trail and followed. He put his pony likewise to the trot. The other man's ears would be filled with the noise of his own progress and so be unaware of pursuit; thus for several hundred yards, then to a slow walk, then a trot. A quarter mile more, and Allan came to a full halt and turned his head. He wasn't far behind the man and he knew he should hear the latter's progress. But he heard nothing at all. Ambush?

Bridle chains jingled close at hand. Well, there was another rider out in this mystery, for Allan made out the man's rapid approach. A short, subdued warning rolled through the night. "All right—pull down, Nuck."

"Where?"

"On the trail."

"Get that boot? No trouble?"

Silence. Allan dropped to the ground and advanced on his toes. Then Nuck Champifer's bullet had spent itself in Lone Star's chest. All the slow anger of the Boadleys flamed up at this fresh fuel. The man ought to die by the same means; he ought to be sent spinning from his saddle and thresh in the sand like a hamstrung lobo. The two of them were talking so softly that Allan made nothing of the words. His gun was out before he raised the bulk of their shadows. A little closer, he could distinguish between those shadows. The smaller one would be Nuck.

"Who follered you?"

"I dunno, Nuck, but I'm feeling it somebody took my trail. Listen—"

A long silence was broken by the impatient Nuck. "What of it? Gimme the boot. I'm putting it on here. That one you lent me is big enough to sleep in." Nuck's spurs rattled as he struck the ground. Allan moved onward with long strides. He should have brought along his loop for this piece of work. Nuck ought to die, but it couldn't be done like that—not while he, Allan Boadley, carried a deputy's star. Now, what was to be done must be swiftly done.

Nuck seemed to be bent half over. The man in the saddle was beyond Nuck's horse sitting quite still. Nuck snapped erect, a challenge in his throat. "What you doing, Cal?"

"Me? Sitting right here on my hunkers. What . . . lookout, Nuck!"

Allan threw his body across three full yards and drove Nuck Champifer before him like a ninepin. Nuck twisted, clawing for his revolver, and in so doing tripped upon his own tangled feet and fell against the barrel of his horse. The horse veered aside. Allan dropped across the prostrate Nuck, chest on chest.

There in the darkness he fought back the vicious, slashing jabs Nuck aimed at his face. The man was small and pinned by Allan's body, but the explosive Champifer temper gave him the destructive power of some cornered feline. Allan felt his chest ripped by five sharp fingers and he sank his forearm into Nuck's gullet like a club. "Stay put or I'll addle your brains!" he muttered. And he managed to find Nuck's gun, hurling it far into the desert.

The puncher on the horse had kept his saddle, making a circle of the two fighters. He kept calling out, "All right, Nuck? I can't shoot 'thout hitting you, Nuck! Got him? Y'all right?"

Nuck's voice rattled shrilly out of his throat. "Get down here, damn your yella heart! Mix in this! It's a Boadley!"

Allan heard the puncher hit the ground. Still holding Nuck beneath him, he twisted and raised his gun at the advancing bulk. "Keep back," he yelled. "I don't want you, but I'll knock you over if you come up!"

The puncher weaved aside and cried, "Hold his arms, Nuck! Hold 'em! Knock down his iron while I pile on!"

"Try it and you're dead," Allan said. "I'm taking this Champifer back to Grail City. Get out of here now before I have to give him a sleep powder."

"You ain't able to make a go of this, Boadley," the puncher jeered. "It's one play too many. Catch hold of his arm, Nuck!" He kept circling. Allan felt the man closing from a blind angle. Nuck exerted a final surging buck and cleared himself partly of the weight. "All right," Allan muttered, "it's your funeral." And he brought the barrel of his gun down flat across Champifer's temple. Nuck ceased to struggle; the puncher had put himself behind his horse. The night was split by the roar of his gun and a blue point of flame gleamed in the shadows. But the bullet was high—necessarily so. Allan threw himself across Nuck's body and raised his gun. "Try that again, waddy, and I'll drop your horse and leave you on your hoofs. I'm holding Nuck against me."

"One good shot, Boadley—"

"Not tonight, fella. Hop in the saddle and fan it. I don't want you. Tell Luke Only his son's in the jug on a warrant for murder."

"Yeah? How long you think to keep him there, huh? We'll knock every damn shanty in the burg to kindling before morning, bub—and have your scalp drying in the wind."

"Clear out. Go break the news."

"You know what it means, don't you?" the puncher persisted. He still kept behind the protection of the horse. Allan saw the animal slowly fade into the darkness, the puncher leading it away out of range. "It means you and all your kind are marked. This day a week from now there won't be any Boadley above the ground. Don't you disbelieve it. We been waiting for a move like this."

Allan kept his peace. He heard the puncher's spurs jingle and presently there was a drumming on the desert, a drumming that grew fainter and died. Nuck stirred out of his sleep, breath uneven. Allan whipped off his bandanna and tied Champifer's hands behind. "All right," he said. "Come out of the dope, Nuck."

"Hey, Cal, where you at?" Nuck grunted, still hazy. "Where's my horse?" Then the realities swept back on full tide and he threshed violently across the sand. "Damn you, lemme loose! What you got on me?"

"A couple of Indian signs," Allan said. "I'm serving a warrant for murder, kid. Something you did over beyond the Medicals a couple of years ago. If that don't stick I've got another murder to pin on your gun. You damned, slinking rat—I'd like to sink you right here! Now get up and mosey! Don't argue or I'll resign my star on the spot and pay off the debt."

Allan pulled him up by the coat and led him along the uneven ground, back to where he had abandoned his horse. Nuck fell to a muttering rage. Now and then he fought at the bandanna and dug his spurs into the ground. At each protest Allan shook him, boosted him bodily across the interval. That evoked the very dregs of Nuck's rage. A scolding bitter profanity poured from his lips. He laughed wildly. He sucked the air into his thin chest like a drowning man.

"You may get me in that calaboose and cut me into bacon strips, Boadley, but by the living God there'll be fifty men riding to blot you yellow scum off the earth before morning! Murder, uh? If you want blood you'll sure as hell get it! We're primed for this!"

Allan reached his horse and flung Champifer up into

56

the saddle, himself mounting behind. "What will be, will be," he replied gravely. "I'm not a killing man, Nuck. I'll hate to see blood spilled. Why, what's the matter with you overgrown fools? Ain't the country big enough for all of us? What did any Boadley ever do to you? Somebody ought to tie you to a wagon wheel and turn the horses loose."

"There never was a good Boadley, never was room enough between you and us," Nuck grumbled. "It's our county and we'll wipe it clean. Don't ever think we won't." He relapsed into sullen silence; nor did he again utter a word in the journey to town. Allan picked up the lights on the Champifer side, made a wide circuit and crossed the river at the south ford. Straight down the street he traveled, and although it was no more than a hundred yards from hotel to jail, he had not reached the latter building when Grail City from bank to bank quivered as if from an electrical impulse; thus swiftly does the blood call sweep across the house tops to warn men. Twenty souls watched Allan pull Nuck out of the saddle and take him into the sheriff's office. And when he had locked the man in the lone dingy cell on the second floor and came back to the street, he saw that almost as many had collected by the bridge on the Champifer side. He beckoned to one of his punchers, issuing a brittle order.

"Get to the ranch as quick as horse flesh will carry. Tell the boys it's come. They've got less than two hours to reach town. Otherwise there won't be any town left. Beat it."

The puncher elbowed through the crowd and went off on a dead run. Allan saw T. Ulysses Gove on the edge of the circle, a thin, obscure figure. And he pointed at the man. "All right, Sheriff. You can collect your party and ride north with him."

"Who?" Gove grunted, looking as if he'd been caught stealing.

"Oh, the time for concealment's all over," Allan replied, somewhat irritated. "Come inside, I want to have a word."

Gove came through the door, closed it behind him and pulled the lone window shade. He tested the lock on the door and with equal caution tried the knob of the back entrance. Then he took a chew and thoughtfully, gravely rebuked the younger man. "Didn't seem necessary to do that."

"You can't be burrowing underground forever," Allan said. "There's your man. You've got first call on him. I've got a call on him, too, for the murder of my father. But I'm not sure I could keep him in one piece when our crew got here. So you better hike out right away and put the miles between town and your next camping spot. If you folks don't convict him, hold him and let me know. I'll bring him back here."

"Nossir," stated Gove, unusually prompt. "I ain't accepting him tonight. Plenty of time. Plenty."

"The hell there is," Allan grunted. "Do you know what's brewing? If you wait till morning you're blamed apt not to have a prisoner. Either they'll get him loose or he'll die from an accidental gunshot wound."

Gove went through all the preliminary motions again. He pared himself additional tobacco, replaced it, removed his hat and massaged a few straggling locks of hair. And he studied Allan with the sadly morose eye of a worldling and a skeptic. "Supposing I should take him tonight? How far you figure I'd get? There's boys watching every move. I been observing a gent sitting on the hotel steps over beyond all evening. Got his eyes glued to this here office. He's a lookout. How far'd I get with said prisoner? Not much more'n you could throw a Hereford heifer by the tail."

"All right—and supposing you haven't got a prisoner by daylight?" Allan countered. "Supposing I can't hold him?"

Gove accepted the situation with a grave shrug of his shoulders. "As between the two eventualities, I'd a blamed sight rather have 'em lift him off the jail than lift him off me. I might get hurt. Now, don't look so damned tight about that sentiment. I'm well along in years and I've seen 'em come and go. Conservation is my motto. I'll claim Champifer at the proper time, which ain't tonight. I'm the first sheriff of my county to live beyond forty-five and I ain't allowing no bad gent to wreck the virtue of all them accumulated years. If he breaks jail, it's too bad. If he dies sudden, it's sad. In either case I'll see the law is plumb satisfied. I always have."

"All right," Allan said.

Cal Levering, the puncher who had been with Nuck,

raced into the Champifer yard and sent three spaced shots up to the sky. Men poured out of the bunkhouses, falling across each other, groping at the buckles of their belts; for such was the tension under which they lived that the sound of a gun was as much as a call to arms. Levering stepped down from the saddle, yelling, "Allan Boadley's got Nuck in the calaboose. Dragged him off his horse on our side of the river. What about it, gents?"

"What for?" demanded one of them.

"Some trumped up murder charge, I reckon," Levering grunted. "What difference does it make?"

Luke Only strode out of the big house, in his shirt sleeves. "What's that?"

"Nuck's in the jug," Levering explained. "Boadley batted him on the coco with the barrel of a shooting piece and drug him acrost the river. Me, I couldn't help none whatsoever."

Luke's jaws worked spasmodically. "What was Nuck and you doing over thataway?"

"Just a pasear, Luke. Just—"

"Come inside a minute," Luke ordered. He swept his arm toward the punchers. "Saddle up. Oil your guns." He followed Levering into the room. The fire on the hearth had died to a few glowing coals. Luke lit a lamp and held it directly into Levering's face. "Now what was you boys doing at Grail City?"

"Nuck had a boot to be fixed," Levering said.

"So you rode slap into trouble," Luke growled. "Serves him right." He ran a bony hand across the metal-blue stubble on his face. It seemed he was grinning, or it might have been only a twist of his lips; whatever the expression, it left this dour and vengeful man's countenance in the mold of a cold, fleering passion. "Get out with the boys!" he snapped. Levering disappeared. Little William came down the stairway, dressed and armed. Susan appeared from a near bedroom. "What was it, Luke?"

"They put Nuck in the jug," Luke Only said. "We're going after him."

"Luke, that will mean war," she protested. "After all that's happened in the last two days, can't you see it will bring nothing but trouble?"

"I been expecting it ten years," said Luke Only. "Now or never. We'll never get a better chance to wipe 'em out."

"Then you want war?" Her face went dead white. "Do you know what Dad would have done to you for that remark? Isn't there a single shred of decency in you? Ever since I was a little girl I've heard you talking trouble. There's death in your blood! I won't have you dragging this ranch into such a mess. Do you hear me, Luke? It's my ranch now. I forbid you to take the men."

He stepped across the space and stood over her, his gaunt black head craned forward on the axis of his skinny neck. She thought for a moment that he meant to strike her, for he half raised a fist. Once again his bloodless lips drew back to a cold, sarcastic grin. "Hear what Nuck told the old gent last night? About us not working for you? That was gospel. It ain't your ranch in anything but name. From now on our word carries the crew. You do what we want you to do."

"You're like a buzzard. If I had a gun—"

"I'll take that out of you soon," Luke Only said. And his open hand struck her on the cheek so hard that she fell back against the wall. Luke swung on his heels and nodded at Little William. "Come on. If they've touched a hair of Nuck's head I'll torture 'em, by God."

Father and son crossed the yard and swung up to saddle. Luke looked back at the shadowed bulk of the crew, silently ranged behind. And there was a kind of savage exultation in his heart, a kind of holy zeal. His time to strike had come. Through all the years he had harbored his bitter enmity, his glowing hatred of the opposite clan, and now he should see them laid down in the dust and all their cattle scattered and their houses burnt. As far as Luke Only was concerned only two colors existed in the universe—black and white, with no intermediate shades. A thing was good or it was bad; it was to be harbored or it had to be wiped out. He was, in fact, a distinct throwback to that period of history when men slew their neighbors out of religious differ-ence and considered that they had done an act of faith. Nothing burns so fiercely as the hatred rising from neighbors arrayed in feud; and Luke Only was the sum total in all his habits and his emotions and his thoughts of the perfect feudist.

So he raised his hand and flung it onward in the direction of Grail City, saying:

"Let's go. Tonight we finish a chore."

They galloped out into the desert.

Susan heard them go. She had, in a moment of wild, hopeless despair, thought of trying to talk the men out of their purpose. That impulse passed. Looking back over the history of the ranch, and recalling the occasional remarks dropped by various members of the crew, she realized now what a volcanic pit her father had built his empire on and how strong he must have been to keep a semblance of peace. He was gone now, and there would be no more peace until one faction or the other was driven from the county.

She ran through the door and toward the corrals. I've got to stop it, she thought. Even if I betray my own blood I've got to stop it! She saddled a horse and galloped after the party, not knowing what she meant to do or where she meant to go.

4. Gove's prophecy comes true

Long before a tornado strikes there are certain premonitory warnings within the atmospheric vacuum cup—a silence as of death or perhaps, far off, a faint and low-pitched droning; and long before a prairie fire sweeps into sight it is heralded by the burnt flakes falling out of the sky. So tonight. An hour passed after Allan Boadley locked the jail door behind Nuck Champifer, and Grail City, though wary and suspicious, was half inclined to believe trouble might not descend upon them. Then all of a sudden, without reason, without any tangible evidence, every soul abiding in the town understood that the cup of destiny was a-simmer and that presently it would boil over, spilling its poisonous brew down the river-split street.

Perhaps it is not quite exact to say there was no reason for this feeling. Cattle land is strung with a thousand unseen wires. The men of cattle land, living against the earth year after year, forever weighing the meaning of small, inconsequent things, alone possess a knowledge of the code that flashes across those wires. By day they might stand on a ridge and read the message of a double puff of dust on the opposite ridge; by night it was the glitter of a man's eyes against the cigarette glow. Or lesser things yet; a tautness that stretched like a band from bank to bank of the sluggish river. Men's hearts beat a little faster, they moved a little slower and the drawl of their speech lengthened, shot with brittle inflections. Old Herod Ames, the saloon proprietor, rubbed a rheumatic elbow—and there was another sign for the Boadley faction to note. Just as the overhead *tonk* of southbound geese tells of winter, so did this Ames's recurrent rheumatism spell disaster. It had, men averred, always been so. There were passing skeptics to doubt this harbinger, to say that in an enlightened age such a belief was only mumbo-jumbo superstition. Thereupon Grail City would recite the roll of trouble that each time followed upon Herod Ames's aching elbow joint. As for superstition, Grail City admitted it; but was not the world a queer, unfathomable place? Surrounded by night and day with the open range, the infinite distance, the very mystery of creation—they knew.

None knew so well as T. Ulysses Gove, who quietly got his horse out of the stable and posted it some hundreds of yards away beyond town in a convenient hollow, himself returning to the hotel. As for Allan Boadley, he swiftly collected the tradesmen and the hangers-on in the hotel lobby. They made a party of fifteen-odd. Most of them were old in the ways of this land, being graduated from the harsher toil of it. They could shoot, they could admirably adapt themselves to any stratagem. Yet Allan, even understanding how rigidly they were bound to the Boadley standard, chose not to take advantage of their loyalty. It was up to them whether they would stay or go; whether they would fight or elect neutrality. This much he told them:

"It's not your quarrel. Some of you punched for my dad when I was in three-cornered pants. Some of you have ridden herd with me. All right. But it's not your quarrel. If you stick here you'll be drawn into it. If you ride off, you're clear."

Herod Ames, the heaviest property owner on the east bank by virtue of his saloon, elected to speak the collective mind. "There's about twenty lowborn counter jumpers t'other side of the crick that's been aping us decent merchants," he said. "We'll take care of that element, Allan. Set your mind to it. Me, I'd love to have a lick at the son of a bald-headed bottle juggler what runs opposition to me. He's set too many rumors afloat regarding the quality of my merchandise. Oh, yeah, we'll take care of them. And we will likewise chip in on the main game."

Gove entered the parley. "Which ranch is closest to town?"

"Champifer house, by about three miles," said Allan.

Gove digested this; the resolution of eternity seemed to wreathe about his cheeks. "Then you had better take some steps toward forting up. That's practical advice—"

A shot echoed up from the river. A slug of lead spat against the lobby stove. Hard upon this came a shrill, penetrating yell. The group unrolled and drew back from the line of fire.

"Ki-yi, you mongrels," Ames muttered.

"Put out the light," said Allan. "It looks as if the battle is on. That's only stray sniping. Main outfit ought to roll in any minute. Turn out that light! Good. Now listen, you boys stay clear of the buildings. Spread out along the river and drop on your bread baskets. They'll expect us to be in the hotel and they'll put a lot of lead in it. If you get pressed too hard fall back on Markowitz's store. One more item. We're apt to get tangled up pretty bad—won't know the other fellow from Adam. So we'd better have some word to pass along. Let—"

"Let it be 'Guns Up!' " broke in Herod Ames, accustomed to this sort of thing. "If the other gent don't answer, why then, suit action to word. Damn 'em, all the vinegar ain't west of White River by a jugful."

"Out of here," Allan said, and led the way. He waited

in the pool of blackness along the porch until they had scattered. "I'll be at the jail," he added, sending his words after them softly. Somebody moved at his elbow. T. Ulysses Gove, it was.

"Ain't got a chew, have you?"

Allan said he hadn't, whereupon the small one displayed the first agitation during his sojourn in Grail City. "Damn the luck! I et the last morsel. It's shore a hell of a time to be shy on tobacco! Where's the store?"

"Listen."

There was no mistaking the sound as it welled across the night air—the drum of many galloping hoofs sweeping onward toward the town. "They've won the first trick," said Allan grimly and pulled Gove across the porch. He ducked down an alley to avoid the store lights and circled through the cluttered back areas to the jail. Once there, he turned down the lamp and walked to the street. The Champifers were riding along the street, on the far side, pair by pair, the line stretching formidably. Allan saw Luke Only in the lead as the latter reined directly in the yellow beam emanating from the saloon. Up came an arm. Luke Only's tinder-dry voice cracked like a gunshot.

"Boadley over there?"

"Waiting for you, Luke," Allan called.

"Turn Nuck loose. Turn him loose in a hurry."

"We've got him on a warrant, Luke. He stands trial for murder."

"By God, he'll never stand trial in Grail County, Boadley! What authority you got anyhow? You ain't sheriff, nor deputy. It wasn't legal. You know it wasn't. I'll give you one more chance."

Allan's fingers brushed the butt of his gun. "I may not be legally a deputy, Luke—but *he's* legally in the jug. And there he stays."

"Then we come after him!" Luke shouted, rising in his stirrups. "And you die!"

"I reckon you'd come anyway," Allan said, sparring for time. He thought he heard a murmur out along the desert. "Would you boys ride back home if I did turn him free?"

"Making no promises," Luke parried. "Turn him loose first and we'll parley afterwards. If you've hurt a hair of his head—"

"Fatherly affection," Allan said, half to himself, "is to be found in queer places. No, Luke, I guess not. You're itching for trouble. But before you cross that bridge say your prayers. There's twenty guns trained dead on you this minute. Remember, no Boadley made a move to start a war. We're dead set against it. I took Nuck in the course of the day's work."

"You took him on Champifer ground," Luke stated. "Which was contrary to the agreement."

"You broke that agreement," Allan argued. "I sent for Old Pierre. Some one of your own crowd killed him. Likewise, your son killed my dad. On top of that you wrote me a challenge. What kind of an agreement are you talking about, anyhow?"

Nuck's shrill voice poured from the jail cell. "Stop that damn talking and come on! Boadley's just augering to save his skin! Break this cracker box down!"

Allan saw the whole Champifer line shift. Luke Only turned his horse toward the bridge, gun raised. "All right, boys, we'll cross over."

"I'm making myself clear," Allan repeated. "No Boadley wants a war. I don't. But we'll fight. You're going to have a lot of empty saddles. Just remember, you're bucking the law when you take a man out of jail."

"Law in Grail County is suspended!" Luke shouted. "Here we come!"

The Champifer line boiled. Allan raised his gun. Luke Only aimed for the bridge, but half a dozen men of his crew preceded him. The boards thrummed to the racing horses, a high and quivering yell rocketed across the water. And then the night was aglow with points of flame, and the roar of successive guns reverberated over all. A bullet caught the foremost horse and it went down, the rider sailing out of the saddle and into the river. The threshing animal choked the narrow causeway, the clamor of voices redoubled. There was a rearing and a plunging of mounts, the gunfire all the while swelling and falling like the echo of a gathering storm. The bridge railing gave way to the pressure, and thus bereft of those guiding marks, men and beasts took the plunge. Allan heard the brazen, triumphant voice of Herod Ames mocking the Champifers.

"Cool off, you damn rascals! It's the first bath you ever took anyhow!"

But the Champifer advance was not checked. Rider after rider flung himself across the planking and swirled down the Boadley side. Allan stood rooted to the jail doorway, and even as he saw them bearing toward him he held his fire. The key to Nuck's cell was in a side pocket. He brought it out and flung it toward the water.

"You'll break the door to get him out," he muttered.

Powder smoke belched in his face. He was nearly ridden over. Somebody leaped far from the saddle, arm outstretched. Allan fired and the horse sheered away, its rider lying still in the dust of the street. The Champifers had split, riding up and down in swift forays upon the various buildings. Being mounted, they made good targets for the Boadley partisans strung along the river bank, and whenever one of these riders passed in front of a ray of light, bullets sang about him. There was danger in this divided marauding. Luke Only, somewhere near the bridge, had seen it and kept calling after his men: "Never mind busting up the furniture. Close up, close up! We got the jail to take first! Come on, boys!"

They came together. Allan felt the whole weight of the party bearing directly upon them. He dropped to a knee and fired at the great shadow they made. The Boadley townsmen seemed to have sensed this situation and were abandoning cover, coming up at the dead run. Bullets smashed through the jail wall, rattled the jail door. Then there was a fresh thrumming along the street—new riders sweeping along out of the desert, past the livery stable and into the Champifer group. The impact of that collision carried the Champifers backward toward the river. Saddle gear groaned, men cried out angrily, iron struck iron. And Allan heard the voice of his brother Snass riding the crest of this maelstrom, strong and unexcited. "Boost 'em, boost 'em! We don't allow no trash dirtying this street!"

The Champifer clan broke; they were disorganized already by the sniping of the townsmen and they hadn't been prepared for the swift and slashing attack that struck them like a thunderbolt. A half dozen hasty ones retreated over the bridge and the sound of their departure shook the more stubborn. The river boiled under their pressed horses as they took the nearest path to safety. The bridge was a lane of death, to be avoided. The townsmen, eased of their burden by the newly arrived Boadleys, had settled to a steady fire that raked every plank of the structure. Some Champifer man out in the middle of it cried in agony and fell still. The rest of the Champifers were collecting on the far bank, Luke Only's voice scourging them with every cruel and stinging word at his command.

Allan called out, "Snass."

"Yeah."

"Get the men in a bunch right here. Better put the horses inside the stable and station a few boys there. But we'll fight afoot. Otherwise we'll knock each other down. Let 'em stick to their ponies—it makes a fair target. Speed it up, they're fixing to make another try. We'll hold this jail until it gets too hot."

"Orders," said Snass. "On the prod, boys. Three-four stay in the stables. Close the doors and watch 'em. Supposing we can't hold this jail, Allan?"

"We'll fort up in Markowitz's then. It's a good shelter."

"Now what—"

The Champifer crew, divided in halves, raced into the darkness, going along the river in opposite directions. Allan ran down the street, lifting his voice to the townsmen. "Get inside—never mind trying to keep up the ambush. They're going to try a nut cracking system." He whirled toward the jail. The men from the ranch were pounding clumsily back from the stable, swearing at the unaccustomed foot work. "Half of you out behind the jail. Three-four inside. Rest stick by me. They've got to take Nuck. It's a scrap now, boys. Save your lead till you see a target. If they drive us too hard cut across to Markowitz's store. All right—here they come!"

The two Champifer wings had forded the stream out in the shadows. Now they flung themselves along the Boadley street, converging at the jail, spilling through adjacent alleys. Luke Only's bitter tongue had scratched hide, for they rode like young buck Indians crazy to make a coup and the high-pitched yell that soared through the dust and the turmoil and the crashing of guns was like a war cry. At the first assault Allan knew they had adopted new tactics. Twenty yards away they dropped out of their saddles and came forward swiftly—part of them aiming at the jail door, part circling to the rear. A dozen bullets ripped through the jail walls. Allan fired at the encroaching shadows, saw dim figures drop and saw other dim figures slide into the vacant spaces. One of his own men—he didn't know who—fell heavily, right at his feet, and died without a word. For that matter, the Boadleys were saying nothing as they stood backed against the jail, parrying the withering fusillade that splintered above and around them. And presently Allan knew it to be an unequal fight. They were being pressed too hard. Somebody caught him by the shoulder and whirled him around and into the jail office. A puncher stumbled after him and slammed the door shut. Snass was muttering, "No use in being lined up to die like that." And he called roll. He repeated two names and got no answer. Allan swore. The slow-stirring wrath of his blood flamed to white heat.

"_____ they'll pay two to one, Snass."

"Yeah, kid. But this ain't the place to fight it out!"

"They'll have to take Nuck. I'm not making any presents," Allan said.

"We ain't paying no fancy prices for him," Snass countered. "We're plumb sunk if they coop us in this two-by-four joint. Come on—we're breakin' out the back way. Markowitz's store is the destination."

"Damned if I do!" Allan said.

Out of a corner floated T. Ulysses Gove's sepulchral voice. "That's the trouble with young deputies—they figger they got to stick to the story book ways. Plenty of time, boy. You can always catch this Nuck person again. Right now he ain't important. I vote to move while we're able."

Snass was already at the back door. "Ready? It's cut and run. Fella that stumbles is lost. Let 'er go!"

The door came open. Out there in the junk-littered rear lots was a row of glimmering blue-tipped lights. Allan was last to leave. Tarrying just a moment in the darkness he heard the front portal swinging on its hinges, then fall to the floor. In poured the besiegers. He took a final shot and slipped after his own men. Somebody's labored breath fanned his face. "Champifer?" He didn't answer, but ducked aside as a bullet tore across the darkness and plucked at his sleeve. He marked the man by the explosion and squeezed his trigger. Snass sent an impatient, worried call down the impenetrable lane, "Allan—hey!" and then ducked onward through the back entrance of Markowitz's store. The spat and lash of guns subsided to a smaller echo. The Champifers had won the second move in this war.

The light was out in the store. Snass was again calling roll, his voice turning methodically down the list. Allan marveled at his brother's calm, for he himself was swept by a furnace heat—he who up to this night had never known what it was to possess a desire to destroy. All about him he heard the hard breathing of the crew. Snass was repeating a name over and over: "Jake Turno—sing out Jake."

There was no answer. Silence closed about the room. A match flared against a cigarette tip, trembling slightly. "Washed out, I'd reckon," someone murmured. "How many's that make?"

"Four," Snass grunted. "But Pinky's only touched. I heard him beller. Guess he got all tangled up with the baling wire."

"Well, there's Ort an' Big Jim with the horses."

"Which leaves Jake Turno to be accounted for."

And after a long, long pause Allan spoke Jake Turno's requiem. "Then it was him that fell in front of me, by the jail door. Dead."

"Pore Old Jake."

"Oh, shut up, you!"

No more shots outside. A Champifer horseman galloped past the store. The clan seemed to be holding a parley by the bridge. Nuck was loose; his sullen, slack voice rose bitterly. "Well, where they at, then? Hell, they couldn't sink in a hole! Come on, come on, let's get organized. The party's only started."

"Mark a score down for that gent," murmured someone sprawled beside Allan.

"Easy—they lost track of us," Snass cautioned, just above a whisper.

Nothing was said for a good ten minutes. Stray sounds came in; somebody stumbled over a box out in the rear and snapped nervously at it. Boots dragged across a sidewalk board. The beleaguered party grew restless. This was like groping down some dangerous hall and expecting a knife to fall. What was up? Water splashed, and it seemed there was a rustling and a scraping on the outer wall of the store.

"Gove," Allan whispered, struck by a sudden thought. "Where's the sheriff?"

Strick Boadley's mutter of astonishment carried across the interval. "Hell, I only got four cartridges left. Say, you fellas count ammunition. This won't do."

"It's funny the town boys ain't here. I told them to fall back to this place. It's damned funny."

"Not funny enough to laugh about," someone replied. "I got six slugs. Which is queer. Had a full belt in the beginning. Don't tell me I shot all them. We only been a minute in the fight."

The imperturbable Snass was checking up. "Average of seven-eight rounds. That's dubious. Ordinarily I wouldn't use ten rounds a season. But the shank of the evening is yet to be et unless I'm a long-haired goat. Markowitz ought to have some cartridges on his shelves."

"No," Allan said. "He let the hardware store have a monopoly on that stuff."

"Which place is a long way off from here."

Robe Boadley, who wasted very few words at any time, sent out a call for gum. It developed that there were none and nobody knew where Markowitz kept it. There was a spurt of conversation in which it became apparent that inaction and suspense were alike hard on the collective nervous system. Nothing developed outside, but the very silence seemed more oppressive and sinister than an open assault. Snass spoke.

"What's orders now, Allan?"

"My bet," said Allan, "is we've put at least six of that

bunch temporarily or permanently out of working order. Odds are still heavy on one end. We can't stay here forever, but we can't go it blind either. That talk we heard sounds fishy to me—sounds like a trick. I'll bet they know where we are. Well, you all stay anchored. I'm going out the back door and cruise a bit. I'll get into the hardware joint and load up on forty-five shells."

Strick Boadley chipped in. "I don't feel gay being divorced from horseflesh. We're too far from that stable by a block. Supposing they've cornered our ponies?"

"No," Allan said. "We'd have heard shooting in such case. Well, I'm on the way."

All this talk had been exchanged at a whisper. Snass had a suggestion. "If you get cornered, space a couple shots to let us know."

Allan crawled to the back door and opened it quietly, an inch at a time. It was as black as the inside of a tomb out there, and as silent. He waited several moments. Then, flat on his stomach, he crawled over the threshold and bunched himself along the sandy earth, heading farther down the rear pathway. Adjoining Markowitz's was the saloon, then a pair of vacant dwelling houses. Next came the hotel, the county court, and at the very end of the row, the hardware store. Originally the county court had been built at the end and a little removed from the rest of the town. But the designers had been over-ambitious and in time it was discovered there were too many rooms to heat and too little business to transact for so great a place. Where-upon the owner of the hardware store, needing space, had swapped quarters with the public officials. Thus, the hardware store rested isolated at one extremity of the street. Allan crawled this way.

Behind the saloon he stopped, hearing the rumble of men talking. A light pricked through a keyhole and he was on the verge of looking into this when some warning instinct stayed him. He drew back. Out beyond, a wire squealed softly. A subdued challenge rolled over the shadows. "Who's that?"

"Got my boot in a damned junk heap, Lip. That you by the saloon?"

"No—"

Allan crept on. The Champifers had thrown a picket line around town and were waiting. He had an impulse to play Indian with them. Shouldn't be so difficult to collect a gun or two. It suited his temper exactly, yet he kept going. Ammunition was the prime necessity at present—and some knowledge as to where the townsmen had gone. He filed the location of those pickets in the back of his head as well as the fact that the saloon seemed to be quartering a crowd of Champifers. Drinking some? Well, that wouldn't help their aim any.

"Well, if it ain't you, Lip, there's somebody by that door."

"All right. You ain't handcuffed any. Go look."

"Me? My life insurance is run out. Oh, hell, I'll go. Champifer yonder?"

Allan was fifty feet removed from the spot and moving quickly. He skirted the back end of the vacant dwelling and reached the hotel. He marked his route by a swill barrel, rose and proceeded on foot. At the court house he stopped again and placed an ear to the wall. This lost him good time. A couple of pickets were roaming along the pathway now and their noise had partly emptied the saloon. Men ran through the street, calling from point to point. Well, wherever the townsmen had gone, they certainly were keeping mighty quiet. Nothing in the court house, apparently; nothing save a lone rat gnawing at a piece of wood. He struck straight across the open lot to the hardware store, figuring to be shielded a little by the general restlessness of the Champifer party. They were patrolling the street; more of them had sifted through the alleys. Something struck the water and across the stream all lights were glowing. The honky-tonk artist in the Champifer saloon was even playing.

"Fiddling while Rome burns. Guess it's all right. He don't own any property here."

"All right—time to start moving ain't it? We'll get no place doing this."

Voices right in front of him. Allan froze where he stood. A shadow marched out of lesser shadows, walked confidently until within five yards. Then the silence seemed to waken the picket's suspicions. "Well, say something! Be damned if all this mooching don't ravel my system! Champifer?"

Allan stepped like a cat. He turned a shoulder and

sprang across the interval. Cloth ripped, a gun spat in his face and pounded on his eardrums. He returned that shot, and was at the back entrance to the hardware store. Why stop to look? The man had gone down spewing words. It was mighty queer how some folks died; bad business to carry a dirty mouth all the way to infinity. He was inside the store, not at all cautious about his movements. Had no time to be; seemed as if Grail City was filled with a thousand men, all yelling. They were coming his way, too. Now where in hell was that shelf of cartridges? He got behind a counter and stopped, closing his eyes to visualize the contents of the place. He'd been in this joint enough to know everything by heart. Ought to be left of a stand of Remingtons. Second shelf up. Couple fish poles hanging on the other side. He stretched his arms and located the Remingtons. From that point he groped across the shelf until he felt the familiar boxes. Somebody ran over the store porch. Others were circling. He had left the back door open and he saw a lantern bobbing up and down and then vanish. They had discovered the dead picket all right. It appeared as if every last Champifer man in the town was jumping this way.

Easy, take it easy, he cautioned himself. Got to get these right. A pocket full of thirty-eight's won't do a bit of good. Yep, those are the proper gadgets.

He rammed a dozen small cartons of them into his pockets—all he could find. For good measure he seized one of the Remingtons and slid his fingers around until he found a box of appropriate shells. And now to get out of this trap.

It was a trap, too. The rear alley was crawling with Champifer men. Therefore, the front door. He stood on the threshold, listening. It might be possible to bluff straight through this. Anything to save time. They were coming out of the alley again—he discovered them advancing toward him. He left the porch and ran down the street, but he heard several men talking and it sounded as if they were blocking his way. Thus hemmed, he stopped a bare instant, or until he began to see the figures of those behind him coming closer. He dropped down the four-foot bank and plastered himself against the sandy shelving.

They came on, ten or more of them. Not five yards from his covert they straggled to a halt while another party slid through the night from an opposite point. Nuck Champifer's familiar voice bit into the grumble and mutter of a stray talk. "Well, what was it?"

"Dode's out. They's a guy roaming loose, Nuck."

"Look in the hardware joint?"

"Yeah. Took a lantern in. Ain't there. Me, I thought I saw him cross towards the river."

"Well, by Godfrey!" Nuck fumed. "This has gone too far! I don't care what Luke says about it, we're goin' to rush every shack on this side till we locate that bunch."

"All right to tell," grumbled another. "But you didn't have to face that first burst of lead. Who said them jaspers can't shoot? Why ram into another play like that?"

"Yellow?" Nuck sneered. "If you ain't got guts enough for this party go on back home."

"You'll get climbed some bright day for shooting off your face like that," said the man. "I ain't yellow, but I ain't half-cocked, either. We've lost seven boys, with blamed little to show for it. How do we know where these gents have got to? Mebbe they're all set for us to stumble into one of them doors."

"I know where they went!" Nuck snapped. "They're in the store. I got an idea. Come on. Where's Luke?"

"By the bridge. How about this guy roaming loose? Might be camping on our heels for all we know."

"Oh, he's probably halfway to the border by now," Nuck said. "Come on, we've got to iron out this wash before morning."

They started away. Allan hoisted himself up the bank, boldly rose and tramped behind them. He looked toward the dim stars and grinned. It was their own idea, not his. Still, this kind of stunt had to be polished off with neatness. And they were angling toward the bridge, which wasn't his direction at all. Luke Only mumbled a challenge. "Cut that cussed noise! You want the whole state should know where we are?" Allan tightened his muscles, dropped out of step and swung away from the party, pacing across the street. The first ten feet, he expected to hear a shout of discovery. The second ten feet, he waited for the bullets to crash around him. Seemed like it was ninety miles to the sidewalk. Markowitz's place was dead in front. He veered slightly to strike the alley. Luke's words barely reached him. "Who told you to draw in the guards—" Allan dropped along the alley. He tapped the wall with his knuckles, hoping those inside would understand the signal. More free information—the Champifer pickets were withdrawn from the junk piles. That left the coast clear. It was high time to move out and make a sally. Daylight couldn't be very far over the eastern rim. He turned a corner, arrived at the rear entrance and felt for the knob. Wasn't there. Door wasn't even there—it stood wide open and a small breeze scoured through. He plastered himself against the boards and the hair ruffled up on the nape of his neck. *"Quien es?"* No answer.

The Boadleys had vanished into the palpitating shadows and nothing was left to mark their course. The sensation to Allan was akin to that of a sailor put ashore on some island to scout the jungle, and later returning to find the ship gone. He felt physically exhausted, and with exhaustion came a moment in which he recognized defeat. The Champifers were too powerful. In the end they would have their own way, which was to uproot all Boadleys, everything that pertained to a Boadley, down to the very headstones on the Boadley graves. Once he had overheard Nuck make that prediction. He laughed at the time and ridden away into the Medicals unconcerned. Well, he had misjudged. Nothing in life, from one end of it to the other, was so powerful as the nursed hate of a feudist. It spanned years and generations and touched the innocent with its bloody mantle.

First the town boys vanish, and now it's the crew, he thought. He reached for his cigarette papers and swore softly when he realized he could do no smoking for a while. And it was that small irritation, that minute pin prick in a night of misfortune, which fed his anger and sent it roaring. He who lives by the sword—well, he'll die, he raged inwardly. By Godfrey, this must be the last war! That unholy tribe has got to be sponged off the slate. I didn't want to start a fight, but I'll see they sleep in a narrow bed before I rest.

He raised his shoulders and stepped away from the wall. The Champifers were launching another bolt. He heard them coming down both sides of the store, coming on the run. Glass shattered and fell somewhere. Nuck's voice, thick with excitement, rose and sputtered. "Hustle, hustle! Damn your hides, the spunk's sifted out of your marrow! I'd trade you for two good sheepherders! Hustle!"

Allan sprang aside. He tangled himself in the loose wire off the junk heaps and went down. Barbed wire that bit him raw. They didn't hear him for they were making plenty of noise. Fighting clear of the wire he reached open ground and ran for the livery stable. He had gone long enough without a pony beneath him; seemed like a man could think clearer off his feet. Somebody signaled shrilly and at that the guns began to crack again and the boards thrummed beneath many boots. Allan reached the stable and put his weight against the sliding door. It rolled open and he fell inside. Instantly he was gripped full around the waist and a familiar voice grumbled, "Where's your calling card?"

"You crazy galoots, what's the idea of pulling out on me?" Allan snarled in relief. So here was the crew again. They had made a dexterous retreat.

"Who's that, Joe?"

"It's Allan."

The ever serene Snass sent a caution down the darkness. "Easy, easy. Allan? By Jim, we figgered you was crossed off the calendar. Well, what's orders? The boys think we've holed in plenty long."

"Gather round," Allan said. "I've got a little sugar."

He broke into the cartridge boxes and distributed the shells. "They're throwing lead into Markowitz's now," he explained.

"I had a hunch they would," Snass said. "Just a hunch. So we inched out the back way when we heard the shooting by the court house."

"We're wasting no more time on this town," Allan cut in. "It's their town. Day's coming and we can't buck a two-to-one proposition."

"Back to the ranch?" Snass queried.

"That would be no better. As long as they can keep us in a coop we're checked. No, my idea is to streak for the Medicals and the timber."

"I don't see it," Snass objected. "If that's orders we'll go. But I don't see it. Our ponies is plenty tired. So'm I. Why should we fog to hell and gone up there?"

"I know that country," Allan explained. "They'll follow. You bet they'll follow. That's what I want them to do. I know a dozen good little traps to pull them into.

Probably they'll run us into some box canyon and set more pickets. If we can just take about ten or fifteen of those boys into camp we can make it a stand up scrap again. That's the idea."

"Sounds better," Snass murmured. "You're the boss, Allan."

"As for tired horses—so are their horses tired. All right. Into the saddles. We'll cut and run."

He followed toward the front of the stable and found a horse he thought was his own. He led it to the doorway. "Up?"

"Up and ready."

Allan stepped into the saddle, pried the door open and sent it along its rollers. "Come on. Save your cartridges."

He sank his spurs and galloped into the street, turned right along the river and followed the compass northward. Behind raced the crew. Not a single Champifer along their path and they had gone fifty yards before the embroiled searchers sent a shout of discovery across the thinning darkness. Bullets whined on both flanks. Nuck's voice was that of a man gone mad. And as long as they were in earshot they had the echo of his raging profanity.

"I'm hit," said one of the crew. "Dunno where." But after a moment's pause he thoughtfully announced, "Can't be very bad, though. I don't feel weak."

They forged ahead, silent, saving strength.

It was not far from dawn when they left the stable. Half an hour later the black curtain to eastward cracked and the sky turned to a pale blue. The land marched away on all sides, barren and undulating. The Medicals towered in the foreground, and presently snow glittered under a full shaft of light. The river ran beside them, the banks falling away, the water shallowing up over sand bars.

"I think they're on the trail," Strickland announced, which was the first word anyone had spoken since the break. Allan scarcely heard his brother for he had his eyes on a juniper tree some distance across the stream. Somebody crouched beneath that shelter. And beyond, another hundred yards, a horse moved, saddled and the reins hanging down.

"Wait a minute—somebody over there in trouble," said Allan.

"We got plenty trouble of our own," Snass argued. But he raised his hand and brought the cavalcade to a halt. The crew dropped to the ground, easing the horses. Allan forded the river and galloped toward the juniper. It was a woman, doubled up. She heard him come and turned over on the sand. Susan Champifer, white-faced, looked up to him.

"My horse shied last night," said the girl, trying to bring energy to her words, "and threw me. I've turned my ankle and I can't reach the beast. There's been shooting in town, Mr. Boadley?"

"It's war," was Allan's grave answer. "Can't put any weight on your foot, ma'am?"

"I've tried. I—I fainted once, so there's no use trying again."

Her hair was out of kilter, falling across one white temple, and she had a smudge on her cheeks. Yet she was fairer than Allan had ever before realized. She was too good for Grail County—and far too good to be tangled with the men of her clan. She wasn't like a Champifer—hadn't she warned him once?—and she had looked him squarely in the face that night with a manner that ever since had plagued him.

"All night in this cold?" Allan said. "Lord! But what were you doing away out here? It's no place to be riding."

She raised her head, a little color came back to her cheeks. "I knew the men folks were meaning to attack you at town. I thought I could ride around and warn you. Oh, don't make any mistake, Mr. Boadley. There's no reason for me to like you or your family. I don't. But bloodshed is something I can't stand. I don't want you or anybody else to believe I let my crew start this. I couldn't help it. Luke wouldn't listen."

"I'll get your horse," Allan said, and galloped off. Grit! She hadn't whimpered, she wasn't sorry for herself. Damn Luke and Luke's spawn! They'd take the ranch right away from her. He caught her horse and brought it back, himself dismounting and putting his arms under her. In all his life he had never so much as touched a woman save his mother. The experience left him hot and cold by turns. "Just lean on me, and keep off that foot. Can you pull yourself up?"

She tried and failed, falling against him. She was

weaker than he had supposed. So he lifted her bodily into the saddle.

"Nothing else I can do, ma'am," he said gruffly. "We're on the march and we haven't got a bite of grub to offer you." He saw dust kicking up away back toward town. "But your folks will be along in a few minutes. They'll take care of you, I reckon."

He was startled at her sudden dissent. "I want nothing to do with them! After last night they'd make life miserable for me! I have no folks now and I haven't got a ranch. I'm sorry, but you'll have to take me along for a while until I can get to friends in the next county."

"Blamed poor accommodations," he said, plainly worried. "We're on the dodge, understand. And we'll be in a fight with your men before the day's out."

"Oh, war, war! Why must men be so blind, so crazy? Well, leave me then. I'll run somewhere—anywhere to get away."

"That bad?" he muttered. "Such being the case, come on with me. We'll fix it somehow. It'll be tough on you, ma'am." He rode across the stream with her and faced the crew. "You boys know this lady. She's trailing with us awhile."

"We ain't taking any women prisoners," Snass objected, quite stiff and formal.

"Not a prisoner. It's of her own free will. Luke has sort of took the reins out of her hands. She's scared to face him. Tried to warn us last night and got pitched off her pony. Sprained ankle."

The crew took this silently, all save the one who had

been touched by a bullet. He protested. "I'm carrying Champifer lead. Champifers have dropped some of us. It don't go easy to have such persons in the party. It ain't fitten."

"I have nothing to do with this war," said the girl. "It was against my will. But I won't impose on you. Thank you, Mr. Boadley."

She started to turn off. Allan hedged around her horse, the meanwhile bearing down upon the wounded puncher with a hot glance. "You keep your sentiments to your own sweet self," he said. "I'm responsible for this lady. She travels with us until she can find better arrangements. All right, let's ride. They're closing up."

Once more they got in motion and struck arrow-straight for the Medicals. On and on they traveled, sullen with hunger and weariness, smarting under the whip of defeat. But Allan was in command now and there were none who wished to cross this yellow-haired man. They had seen him in a rage, and they knew how glowing hot, how slashing was that temper when the bridle was removed. So they kept the peace, not a one of them looking at the girl. Snass bore off a little from the column's head and let Allan take the lead. The girl rode beside Allan, and from time to time, when he saw her struggling with some fresh twinge of pain, he drew in to lay an arm across her saddle by way of reassurance.

They struck the first fringe of stunted jack pines, left the river's course and climbed into the speckled shade. The sun veered toward the ceiling of a bright and cloudless sky. Dust rose thicker behind. The Champifers were closely pursuing and gaining somewhat.

5.   Dodge and fight

High up in the Medicals, the Boadley cavalcade came to a halt. For better than two hours Allan had led the party on through the scattered pines, along deep draws thick with brush, across ridges and farther into the wilderness. It was punishing on all of them, especially so with Susan Champifer. Yet neither she nor any of the crew protested, for this was a country Allan knew better than any other man in Grail. Year after year he made his pilgrimages into these hills, leaving the range riding for others. And at present he seemed to be seeking some favored spot. When he signaled for a stop it appeared he had not yet found it; but there was water brawling down the draw and a scattering of red huckleberry bushes ripe with fruit. Food and water. He traced along the creek bank with his finger.

"Deer track there—fresh. It'll be blamed poor venison and out of season. But we can't choose. Strick, you go knock that animal over. Time to eat."

It was quite shaded here and the pines trooped thickly along the slopes. A single vista led downward toward the flat country and stopped, within a hundred yards, where the trail made a turn. Some forest bird streaked across the still air with a chattering voice and a flash of scarlet. Allan wiped the sweat from his face. "Doc and

Bill, you walk back on the trail a couple hundred yards and hide in the bushes. Bo Ambler, take a pasear over on that left ridge. There's an old trail some of those boys might know about and use to sneak up on us. Get going. Now, about a quarter mile straight up this gulch is a bald knob. You can see straight down the slope and along the clearings. Rixey, that's your committee. They'll have to cross some of those clearings whichever way they come."

The appointed men went off. And the rest withdrew up the ravine, leaving the girl alone with Allan. She noticed this with a sad turning of her head. "They have no use for me. I shouldn't have let you bring me."

"Where would you have gone?"

She answered this with a slow turn of her wrist. "Do you know," she went on, "you are not the kind of a man Nuck kept saying you were."

"What kind of a man?" he demanded.

But she wouldn't answer that and so he turned to another matter. "We'd better do something about that foot. Looks kind of puffed to me."

"It's hurt so long I'm almost used to it. There's no use trying to pull the boot off. It won't come."

He took out his knife and slit the leather of the boot down to the ankle bone. Beyond that point he had to be a little rough. Susan's hands curled into each other and tightened. She looked up toward the trees, her head thrown back, her nether lip between her teeth. "Good girl," Allan approved. "Hurts like original sin, don't it? I guess grit runs in your side of the family. My dad told me a yarn about your dad having a bullet dug out of his shoulder. Old man bit into a chunk of wood and said, 'Pull the damn thing and don't stop till you get it.' I guess that—"

The boot came off. Susan relaxed. "My dad—" she began and then started to cry. Allan didn't know whether his words had done it or the pain. But he closed his mouth and swore at himself for being a tactless fool. "Never mind," she said, getting control of herself once more. "A woman can't help being weak. I don't blame your men for not wanting me along."

"My men are all fogged. Don't pay any attention. But you see, we'll be shooting at your flesh and blood—and it don't set good with you around to watch that."

"*My* flesh and blood," she repeated bitterly. "I've got much to thank them for." And her manner of saying it made him look up. She was dead white and her eyes were quite hard. "If I had a gun and Nuck were to be in range I'd shoot him. So much for my flesh and blood."

Allan got up and went over to his horse. He wondered, as he unlashed his blanket roll and pulled a kettle from it, what she knew of Nuck's part in Old Pierre's murder. How could she know anything about it? He went to the creek and filled the kettle, came back and started a small fire of dead sticks. Over this he propped the kettle. "It'll be hot in two-three minutes. You soak that foot some good. I'm going up to parley with the boys."

He found them stripping the huckleberry bushes. Removing his hat he fell to the same chore. And while doing this a solitary gunshot echo rolled down the slope. The whole crew straightened and for a little while were watchful. By and by Strick came back with a skinny buck deer over his shoulders. "All bone and ligaments," Strick announced. "But I'm plenty hungry enough to eat hair and hoofs."

They lost no time in cutting the animal and putting the steaks over a quick flame. Snass reached across the fire, took what he regarded as a choice piece of meat from one of the men and silently passed it to Allan. That was Snass's way of conveying his apologies to the girl. Allan grinned at his elder brother and went back to Susan. She had finished with the hot water.

"Venison for substance, huckleberries for dessert. Fall at it, ma'am."

She looked at him in such a manner that he felt embarrassed. "What would I have done alone?" she murmured. "I'd rather have you call me Susan."

"That works the other way around," he said.

"All right—Allan. But remember, I'm not supposed to be a friend of yours."

Allan remembered an identical phrase in the anonymous note and it made him grin. "Seems I've heard or read that before."

That caught her off guard. She colored and for a moment he thought she was about to grow angry. But she didn't. Instead she lectured him. "A woman may take advantage of a man, Allan. But a man may never, never take advantage of a woman."

"That's right," he drawled. Few people could withstand the man's grin. Susan tried to, but failed. She smiled a little wryly and set about her meal.

One of the guards came lumbering up the trail all in a sweat. In front of Allan he dropped to his haunches. "Saw 'em strung out in the trees some considerable below us, Allan." He looked wistfully at the huckleberries. "Can't make out what they're doing—but they ain't moving very doggone fast this way."

Susan offered him the huckleberries, "Help yourself."

"No. Oh, no, thanks," said the man. "Me, I'll pick some. Don't you go offering nobody nothing around this half-civilized bunch." He looked inquiringly at Allan. "Reckon I'd better amble back, uh?"

"No, go get some of that venison," said Allan. "Have Snass send a couple new boys down."

Snass was calling over to Allan. "Rixey's back from the bald knob. Says they're moving all over the landscape. Don't seem to have any direction."

"Time for us to pull freight, then. Back to saddles."

The guards were pulled in and the group swung up once more. Allan gave Susan a lift and led off with her beside him. This Snass kept his place, and he unbent so far as to say, very gruffly, "I'd favor that limb as much as I could, miss."

"Thank you."

The afternoon shadows lengthened and still Allan followed the narrowing defiles toward the summit of the range. Every mile or so he changed his course. The sun sank and almost instantly it was cold, with the blue shadows swirling around them and a wind rolling down from the remote snow-crusted peaks. They fell into a canyon with great walls sheering up on either side. Allan marched toward the head of this, following an old trapper's trail. Strick, who had lagged, came galloping to the fore. "They've thrown a line acrost this blamed canyon. What's ahead of us, Allan?"

"Nothing much but a plain wall, Strick. Straight up and down."

"Well, by Jim," Snass said. "Y'mean we're boxed?"

"For the time being I guess you might say that," Allan drawled. He veered and in the darkness struck another trail crawling upward. It was a stiff grade. The weary line lengthened. Of a sudden the rock walls seemed to relent and open up. They were under an immense shelving. Water trickled out of the heart of the granite formation and splashed softly beneath the horses' feet.

"We camp here," said Allan.

A murmur of relief ran along the line. Allan dropped to the ground and lifted Susan off her saddle. In here it was quite dark, yet he proceeded down a natural corridor as if he knew it by heart. Presently he set her gently on the loose rubble. "Back in a second," he said.

The girl struck her boot into the shale and by way of experiment took a small rock and threw it as far as she could. There was a remote echo. Allan came back, touched her in reassurance and spread a pair of blankets. "Sleep here. No supper tonight and no prospects.

What's the difference? We ate too much meat anyhow. Well, good night."

"Two blankets, Allan? That means you sleep without any. No, I won't. Take one back."

He lied smoothly. "Had an extra one in my roll."

Her hand touched his shoulder and rested there a while. "Good night, Allan. If I dream at all tonight it will be of you."

"No such luck for the wicked," said Allan. The arm dropped and he groped away. A match flared in the distance, a yellow bomb of light. A gaunt, stubbled face was for an instant outlined. The girl fell asleep with the murmur of men's voices lulling her. Out there by the mouth of the rock fault the Boadleys were holding another parley.

The first thing she heard was a question. One of the crew was grumbling about his stomach. "What's for breakfast?"

And the answer was, "Pure mountain water, you galoot. What more do you want? How can a gent be so blamed particular?"

Susan sat up in her blanket. She had slept well into the morning, for the full hot light came pouring along the vault. By daylight it stood revealed in all its massive proportions, as some ancient cliff temple. Long ago the uneasy earth had rolled like the sea, to create the rugged ridges along the whole range, and that same upheaval had fashioned this immense opening. It was a good forty yards to the entrance, narrowing as it proceeded into the heart of the rock; back of her it continued a still greater distance and was lost around a bend. All the horses and all the crew were harbored in the place, yet it could have held as many more inhabitants without being crowded. Looking past the men, she had a clear view across the canyon to the opposite wall.

Allan had seen her moving and came back, his hat set at a cheerfully rakish angle. He looked worn and there was a two-day stubble on his face, but still he maintained his bubbling humor. "Feel some better?"

"I never heard anybody talk about this place before," she said. "How did you find it?"

"Used to be an Indian hangout in the old days. They weren't telling white people, but an old red guide told me. Blame few white men ever traveled this canyon and when they did they missed the trail up the slope. Come on out and I'll show you the sights."

He half lifted her from the blankets. Supported on his shoulder, she went down the corridor and came to the opening. The men were scattered loosely on the floor, crosslegged and taciturn. Snass was out at the very rim, flat on his stomach and watching something way below. The trees clung tenuously to the sharp incline, ranging all around the mouth of the cavern and thus screening it from sight. At first she failed to see any possible way of reaching this covert, so closely did the rocky aperture merge with the sheer walls of the canyon. Presently Allan pointed out a thin trail that skimmed along the earth.

"Did we come up *that?*" demanded the girl. "Why,

one foot was all that kept us from falling!"

"Not if you let a pony have his bit. See anything, Snass?"

Snass nodded. "Right through them two dead stumps—see? Looks like they got three-four men on picket. I bet they dunno where we are yet."

"We'll have to let 'em know pretty soon," Allan said.

"What for?" Snass grumbled. "They got the mouth of the canyon shut. Why advertise our poor sense? Only way we can pull out of this mess is to climb straight up and over, which means leave the horses. It ain't a pretty situation, Allan. What was in your mind, anyhow?"

"Plenty." Allan turned to Rixey, that one of the crew who had been on lookout the preceding day. "Didn't you say it appeared as if they were all scattered along those clearings? Yeah. Did it look like all of 'em were coming?"

"I never got sight of more'n ten or fifteen at a time," Rixey said.

"Well," Allan said, "They ain't pressing us very hard and it seems to me some of that gang deserted the ship. Looks as if there's just a small guard left to keep us boxed and starve us. My personal opinion is, some of them have gone back to town for grub and fresh horses."

"It's a risky experiment to go down on that idea and fight it out," said Snass.

"I'd just as soon," Rixey grumbled. "I could eat, too."

This brought a scattered protest from the others. "My

God, Rixey, can't you keep your mind off your stomach a while?"

"Between meals I can," Rixey argued. "But it ain't natural to miss so many in a row. Supposing a gent's stomach should shrink? A fine how-de-do."

"Considering what a hog you have always been at table," countered another, "it wouldn't hurt you none to shrink a little."

Allan crawled beyond Snass and got a foothold in the rocks leading upward toward the summit of the ridge. "I'm going to get a good view down there."

"It's in rifle range," Snass cautioned. "Don't put yourself in a place to be knocked off."

Allan disappeared. The sun swung up and the hillside became hot. The girl retreated a little while the rest of the crew fell to a brooding silence. It was a good two hours before Allan slid back down the incline. "I'm right. There's only about twenty of 'em left, as best as I could judge."

"Rest might be somewhere near at hand," Snass objected.

"It's a hunch I've got," Allan said. "I'll play it."

The crew brightened at the thought of action. Snass alone protested. "Minute we start down that trail we're open to fire. Supposing we do make it and close with those boys. They've got plenty trees to hide behind. Mebbe we can overcome that, too, but what's the assurance Luke and Nuck ain't laid a trap with the other half we can't discover?"

"Why go down the trail?" Allan grinned.

Snass moved impatiently. "Climbing up the slope ain't no better. They can spot us and be plumb ready by the time we get within revolver range."

"Why go up the slope?" Allan parried.

"You ain't got any wings which I can see," Snass said.

"I want twenty of you fellows. Rest stay here on guard. While we're gone, make a fire or something so they can spot you."

Snass was wholly skeptical, but he only raised his shoulders. "You're the doctor."

Alan told off the men he wanted, leaving Snass and four of the crew behind. Rixey, one of those so abandoned, felt hurt about the matter but covered it with a suggestion they bring back some grub. Allan turned directly into the cavern. "We may be gone till dark. You boys don't move, no matter how much firing you hear."

"What you going in there for?" Snass asked.

Allan was fifty feet along the rock corridor, half obscured by the shadows. "Because, old timer, there's a tunnel leading right on through the ridge to the other side. Just big enough to wiggle along."

"Well, by Jim!"

"Didn't I tell you once I knew these hills? I picked this canyon for a purpose." Then he was lost to the girl and those men left on guard. The narrowing vault swallowed the whole party. Snass looked toward Susan. "Every time I figger Allan is doing a fool stunt he springs a surprise on me. That boy is too good for this dried up county."

Allan had reached the point where he was down on his hands and knees. The labored breathing of the following crew reverberated from the constricting walls of the tunnel. It was as dark as the inside of a sealed cask, it was a-sweat with cold moisture, and from time to time a loose bit of rubble fell with a dismal clanking sound. Save for, Allan, not one of the party had the remotest idea as to where they were being led, and this kind of subterranean progress was enough to shake their nerves. There is no fear so hard to control as the fear of being trapped underground.

"I don't see no light ahead," Strick Boadley muttered.

"You won't for a good spell," was Allan's answer. He was down on his stomach, crawling an inch at a time. And still the passageway grew smaller, until outcropping bits of rock hooked into his shirt and he had to stop and cautiously disengage himself.

"Why did you leave Snass behind?" Strick asked, more to hear himself talk than for any other reason.

"Because he's about ten pounds too big to get through."

That woke a strangled protest somewhere in the rear. "Is this thing that narrow? Why didn't you tell us before we started? Me, I'm ready to turn around right now."

"Double on that," groaned someone else. "I'd rather be shot than crushed."

Allan tested the hole as he progressed, both arms stretched ahead. There was no other way he could move, for his shoulders were occasionally flush with the side of the tunnel; and somewhere along that blackness he was forced over to one side to double around a sharp bend. He sent a warning back at this point.

"Take it easy when you cut this corner. It's a little bit sandy and blamed damp."

"Say, Allan, you ever been through this before?"

"Once."

A long silence, and then an uneasy rejoinder. "Well, once ain't enough. Supposing she's blocked? How the hell are we going to get back?"

Someone in the middle of the party began to swear in mortal distress. "Hey, I'm wedged! Gunbelt hung on something. Damn it, I can't move!"

"Stop that!" Allan shouted. "Take it easy. This is no place to start a stampede. Inch around until it's free. You boys want to rest?"

"Hell no—go on!"

Another bend and a bell-like opening. Allan crossed this quickly and struck a second narrowing stretch. This was, as he remembered it, the most difficult part of the tunnel. And for all his cheerful temper he began to sweat immoderately. There ought to have been a point of light up ahead, and there wasn't. Going forward was one thing; backing up feet first was entirely something else. He jammed both shoulders against the tunnel and developed a small panic. His impulse was to fight—and that he would have done save for Strick's sudden words. "Being buried alive can't be worse'n this, kid. Next time I go on your party I want specifications. How much longer?"

"Not much," Allan said, getting a good tight hold of his mental state. He passed the narrow point, turned another right angle and felt like shouting. Broad daylight ahead. And wasn't it curious how comforting a thing daylight was? Plenty of room here. He got to his hands and knees, lumbering like a locoed steer. He should have waited a moment at that point and scanned the surrounding forest, but he didn't. He fell out of the tunnel on all fours, rolled down a six-foot slope and came to a full stop in a grass bowl. A chipmunk scolded him from a tree limb.

"That's right," he said, grinning like a fool. "Don't you ever imitate the lowly mole. Stick to your own element."

One by one the crew came rolling out of the cavern's mouth and down into the bowl. They were an odd-looking set, smeared with mud and laboring to keep some self-respecting amount of impassivity upon their faces. And one by one they rose from the ground, clawing for cigarette makings.

"Wait a minute," Allan said. "Where's Bill?"

At that instant the designated puncher came scrambling through the aperture and pitched head first into the assembled party. He turned over, shook himself and stared wildly about. "G-got stuck. Thought I was dead. Even heard a harp playing and St. Peter muttering to hisself, 'Bill Baines? No sech name on my list. Try the opposition.' G-gimme a cigarette."

That was the spark to set off the accumulated nervousness. They shouted, then groaned, they struck each other and the small bowl rang with the wild, unmusical glee. Allan waited patiently, wiping the dirt from his face.

"When you're through with the hysterics we'll proceed."

"Where we at now?" Strick asked.

"Back side of the ridge. There's a little canyon below those trees which angles toward the mouth of the big canyon. Runs into the place those Champifers are stationed. Come on—and take it easy. Be in hearing distance pretty soon."

He led off, ducking into the trees. The party followed single file along an overgrown trace, stumbled around barriers, struck through occasional dense tangle of thicket. The trees marched to the very edge of a creek where the party stopped to drink. They went on again, trudging patiently in pursuit of Allan who seemed unable to keep a straight course more than three minutes at a time. It was this way and that. The creek disappeared, the brush almost overwhelmed them. They went uphill, doubled back and went downhill. A porcupine rolled across their path and wistfully every eye followed that quill-jacketed slow-poke of the forest. An eagle floated high in the heavens, the trees thinned. Allan raised a warning arm. Away down an alley of the canyon side they saw a Champifer partisan crouched behind a stump. With infinite caution they treaded on into heavier shelter and halted.

"What now?" Strick muttered.

"That gent is one I saw from the top of the ridge,"

Allan said. "It's a sort of outpost. They've got three-four such places and send men out to keep up the scout. The main bunch, best I can figure, is behind those pickets—about fifty yards in the brush. We'll skirt them and come up from behind. Then circle them and demand a surrender. Meanwhile, I want one of you boys to slip along toward that fellow and get a bead on him. When we raise a shout, you take him."

"My meat," said Bill Baines, and swung off into the foliage like the sorefooted pedestrian he was. One of the party observed that limp with gloomy foreboding. "You can't take a gent off his pony and not do mortal injury. Me, I'll never be the same."

Allan signaled and they followed, treading the earth more carefully, traveling slower. Westward, the sun was ready to sink below the rim and already a kind of cobalt twilight swirled beneath the tree tops. Once they had sight of the canyon wall with the last blood rays of the day turning the striated earth to a patchwork of vivid coloring. Sunlight there, shadow here. And the smell of wood smoke tainting the air.

They skirted a meadow on all fours, dodged through a patch of fire-killed snags, and once again halted in the shadows. Talk came murmuring along the air and they saw a camp fire shuttering through the leaves. Allan flung his arms wide and brought them together in an embracing gesture. The crew deployed and sank from sight. Allan crept ahead, keeping contact with those men immediately to his right and left. Flat on his stomach he parted a scrub bush and had full view of some fourteen of the Champifer partisans idling on the ground, forty feet ahead. They were in a kind of natural bay. Beyond them was another stand of seedling pines, and beyond that the canyon floor swept straight out and upward. Fourteen men—but Allan, observing eighteen tethered horses, knew four men to be out on duty. One of those he had sent Bill Baines to cover. He must take his chances with the remaining three. Even as he watched, a puncher ducked through the seedlings and squatted on the ground. Another of the party slowly got up, evidently ready to take his turn. One more man in the net. Allan made a swift calculation of the elapsed time and looked to either flank. He rose to a knee, brought out his gun and filled his chest.

"Let 'er go!"

He raced into the little clearing, his crew erupting from the brush at all angles. "Up on your feet! Hands skyward! First to jerk a gun is first to die! Stand pat!"

The Champifer party seemed sucked into the vortex of a whirlwind. They sprang up, startled from the long lethargy of waiting. They weaved irresolutely. A pair started off at a dead run and stopped within a yard of the Boadley ring.

"Boxed!"

"Up—up!" Allan yelled. "By Godfrey, this ain't a time to make a false move! You—get 'em up!"

One lone Champifer puncher reached for his weapon. A double explosion filled the little bay and the puncher dropped soundlessly. Strick was bending forward, yellow head bobbing from side to side, a trace of smoke purling from the muzzle of his piece. He laughed and the echo of it broke flatly across the open space. Allan noted one of the trapped faction turning slowly on his heels; and at each quarter revolution the man muttered, "All right, we're licked. All right, chips is yours." His eyes reached Allan and stopped. "How'd you get out of that canyon, I want to know?"

"No parley," Allan said. "All of you gents put your backs to me. Hustle—no time to lose. That's right. Strick, you go forward and jerk the irons." He was ferreting the group with a skipping glance. "Where's those three red Indians you men work for?"

"They'll be back plenty soon," grumbled the Champifer spokesman.

Strick went at his chore, flinging the captured guns in a pile. Allan sent a pair of his men on through the seedlings with a gesture. "See can you locate the other two. See what Bill Baines is doing."

"All fixed," Strick reported.

"Take three-four lariats from those saddle horns. Half hitch around every one of these gent's windpipes and double knot on the wrists. You boys pitch in and give Strick a hand."

The Champifer spokesman turned to Allan. "Better handle us easy, Boadley. Our turn will be coming. Don't lay no bad debts agin yourself."

"What's the matter with Luke and Nuck?" Allan jeered. "Don't they do any personal fighting? What do you boys get for scorching your hands on their chestnuts."

"Aplenty. You got a star on your vest, Boadley? Well, take it off. It won't mean a thing by sunset."

Bill Baines came limping through the seedling pines with his prisoner. "Say, found any grub among this crowd?" There was a shot out beyond, and presently the search party came back empty-handed. "Got away—a couple of 'em. Ran like a pair of Eyetalian gazellas. No, I wouldn't run on my bunions to catch the golden fleece."

The job of improvised shackling was done. "Back we go," Allan said. "Lift your feet and don't stop to pick any flowers."

He stayed in the little clearing until the last of his party had left. That heap of guns wouldn't help him. The horses would, but there was no time to take them. It was a skip-and-run affair. The other half of the Champifer outfit might have been near enough to hear the scattered shots. And he wanted to put his prisoners well up in the timber before Nuck and Luke arrived. For the next few days, more or less, those captives would be lost to the world. Fifteen men cut away from the Champifer roll left thirty-one to contend with. And from that number there were some casualties to be deducted.

Give them thirty for good measure, Allan mused. That makes it almost an even scrap. We can sally out now and trade swaps. Blamed if I know what we'll feed the guests we got. Have to hunt more huckleberries, I'd reckon.

His eyes fell upon the dead man just as he was about

ready to leave the clearing. He pursed his lips, swearing softly. There was something pretty definite about death. There the fellow lay, cut down like a grass shoot before a sickle. And a moment ago he had been alive with God only knew what hopes and what vital promptings. That was a sample of a feud's long, blighting arm. It wasn't fair. Better a Champifer had never been born than to cause all this waste. He struck after the party.

It didn't do us any good to kill that fellow, Allan thought. He's only a white chip in the game. There won't be any peace until Luke and Nuck die. By Godfrey, they've got to die!

All of a sudden night flung the edge of its mantle across the canyon and the forest. A night breeze sprang up and the world was left to the smaller creatures. And Susan would be sitting up at the cavern mouth, her clear, wistful face tilted toward the star-dusted sky. It wasn't fair!

Allan caught up with his party. They were groping uncertainly beneath the trees. He led them over the tortuous ground, gliding like an Indian. This was country he knew well enough to travel with closed eyes. Once he stopped to listen. He thought he heard brush crackling below and the whinny of a horse.

An hour later he brought the party to some unknown spot high on the ridge. He left half of his men to guard the prisoners. The other half he took with him, crossing the summit of the ridge and crawling down the precipitous farther side. Presently he was hailed sharply.

"Allan—Snass."

He dropped to the rock shelving, once more back at the cavern's mouth. A hand touched his arm lightly, Susan's voice trailed vaguely out of the soft darkness. "Allan—was anybody hurt?"

"One of your punchers, Susan. God knows we didn't want to. He wouldn't stay put. It ain't him we want, it's—" The rest of it stuck in his throat. After all, she was a Champifer. Her blood ran in the veins of the two he meant to wipe out. So he stood still, staring across to where her shadow was framed against the lesser blackness.

"I know, Allan. I know—"

Snass broke in. "Look down there. Guess they're fixing up for the night."

Allan turned about. A fire gleamed below and beyond, somewhere in the canyon's mouth. By that token he knew Nuck and Luke Only had returned. A shot rolled across the distance.

6. Defeat

"What happened?" Snass asked in a far-away voice. Allan told him. Snass murmured something in the darkness. "Then we're almost even Steven with that bunch. Can go out and swap slug for slug. Some more boys has got to die. Seven-eight gone already and all of 'em good hands—yeah, good hands. They ain't the ones that had ought to take the long sleep." Allan never before had heard his brother so philosophically minded. Snass moved, speaking to the girl. "You'll excuse it, ma'am, when I say that they's only two which deserve to die—Luke and Nuck. They're the rotten apples in the barrel."

The girl said nothing at all. Snass cleared his throat and rumbled on. His arm made a vague arc toward the sky. "Been sitting here all day like a Hindu fortune teller, watching up there. Sure gives a man a new slant. This fevered earth ain't a drop in the celestial bucket. Not a drop. Every last one of us is just a flash in the pan. Like that." And he snapped his fingers. "Why should we be fighting when they ain't hardly time to live and enjoy? I never wanted no war. None of us Boadleys wanted war."

"Neither did my father," said the girl. "All his life he struggled to keep the peace—that is, as long as I knew him."

"Old Pierre was a strong gent," Snass agreed. "A fair gent after his fashion. He and Lone Star was two of a kind. One lesson was plenty for them. But Luke and Nuck ain't the kind to learn."

"I think I'll go to bed," Susan murmured.

Allan helped her back into the cave. She rolled into the blankets. "I should never have put myself on you folks," she said. "What you must do, you must do, and I'm only making it harder. It isn't fair."

"You've been a good sport," Allan protested. "You haven't said a word. Why worry?"

"I know. But all the while you're thinking of me and my blood. Naturally, being a woman, I don't want to see this war continued. And however I hate my uncle and my cousin I couldn't ever bring myself to wish their death. You know it, whether I say anything or not. Oh, I wish I could do something to stop it!"

"More men must die first," Allan said. "It's written in the books. Those two won't stand for peace. They've got an itch to erase us. It's been in their minds too long. Either they go down or we go down." He rolled a cigarette and lit it. The girl saw his face outlined a moment, harsh and drawn. "But I'll make you a promise, Susan—"

"No! I don't want you to make me any promise! It isn't fair to bind yourself. I won't take them!"

"I make you a promise. When the time comes for Nuck to face me, and when we start to draw—that's comin' as sure as grass grows and water runs—I'll let him draw first."

"Oh, Allan, I don't want *that* promise! You must take care of yourself!"

"Why—what difference does it make?" he asked, genuinely surprised.

"Don't you see? No, of course you don't. Here I am, a Champifer among Boadleys—wishing, wishing. Go away, Allan!"

"Good night. This thing will be settled before very long." He groped back to the cavern entrance. Snass smoked thoughtfully.

"Have to keep a guard tonight," he announced. "What's orders now, Allan?"

"I'll draw most of the crew back here just before

dawn," Allan said. "Leave only three or four to watch the prisoners."

"If we aim to brace 'em, we'd better get off this ledge."

"Those prisoners are about as much of a handicap as a help," Allan said reflectively, watching the light of the distant fire. Another gunshot echo unraveled along the canyon. "It makes the fight fifty-fifty. But supposing Luke and Nuck decided not to fight. Then what? We can't keep prisoners forever. Supposing all hands agree to a truce. Then we give the prisoners back. Which will give them the edge once more—and they'll start the scrap all over. Complicated."

"There won't be no truce till them two Champifers is dead—or we are," Snass stated.

"It's my belief," Allan agreed.

For the rest of the night they kept a watch on the ledge. Around midnight Allan caught a few hours' sleep, to be up again directly before daylight. He made his way up the canyon side and back to where the prisoners were stationed. And when the first pale violet rays of false dawn came seeping above the eastern rim, so that it was light enough for fewer men to stand guard on the collected Champifer partisans, he left three of his own crew behind on this duty and brought the rest back to the ledge.

"We'd better move down," Snass said.

"I'd thought of making another little foray like the last one," Allan said, "but they'll be watching for just that trick. Anyhow it won't do much good to capture

114

them. I've got a warrant for Nuck, but in the end we'd have to let all the rest go. We've got to work it some other way. Trouble is, Snass, there ain't enough cover down in the canyon for us. They've got the forest to hide in. All we'd have is the bare floor and a few rocks."

"We'd better move somewhere," Snass insisted.

"Well, in case they force the issue we can move out our back door again," Allan drawled. "It's still a mystery to them."

Bill Baines's fervent remonstrance whipped back at him. "Not on your grandmamma's tintype! I'll jump, I'll climb or I'll swim, but I'm eternally damned if I crawl through that chamber of horrors. I'd rather herd sheep."

Sunrise came all of a sudden, and with it arrived the first sign of activity among the Champifers. Two shots, evenly spaced, woke the echoes. Allan, peering down the slope, saw a strip of white cloth waggling rapidly.

"Somebody wants to talk," Snass grumbled.

"Think I'll go meet the gent."

"Now listen—" Snass began.

He was interrupted by the girl, who had come from her shelter. "Allan, never turn your back to my cousin—if it's him."

Allan dropped off the ledge and followed the narrow trail downhill. He passed a few scattered pines and recognized Nuck Champifer crouching in the shelter of an eroded boulder.

"What'll it be, Nuck?"

"I'm alone," Nuck said. "Fair play. Come down farther. Want to talk."

Allan descended to within ten yards of the man and dropped to his heels. Nuck lowered the flag and his black, shifting eyes passed along Allan's body. "Pretty smart maneuver, Boadley. Pretty smart. But it don't buy you no groceries. Where's my men?"

"Tied, labeled and neatly stored away," Allan said. He grinned at Nuck's sudden fury.

"You murdered one," Nuck growled. "That's another score on the slate. I want them men and I want 'em in a hurry. See?"

"You're a poor hand to bluff, Nuck. Why try it? Right now we're even. We'll fight you down to the last cartridge, if that's what you want."

"On an empty belly?" Nuck jeered. "You're licked, Boadley. I hold the trumps. All of 'em."

"Well, we hold half of your crowd," Allan said. "Digest that."

"You won't hold 'em long," Nuck retorted. "Got your deputy's star on your person? If so, throw it away. It ain't no good. I appointed you deputy and I'm discharging you from same position."

"Since when?"

Nuck played his first trump right there. "Since last night, Boadley. We held another election in Grail yesterday and I'm sheriff. Smoke it, mister."

"Another comic opera election," Allan said. But that put a new face upon the whole situation. Nuck held the whip. "It's as good an election as any held in the last fifteen years," Nuck countered. That, too, was near the truth. "Now, Boadley, I want you. I hold a warrant for your arrest—for the murder of Old Pierre Champifer. You may fight me and my men all day long, but it'll do you no good to fight the authority of the county. If you do, I can call out as many special deputies as I want and legally exterminate you. Don't doubt I'll do it, either. Surrender?"

"Who signed that warrant?"

"Judge Addis."

"The judge always was a little partial to your family. Well, it's neat, Nuck. I'll admit it's neat. So you want me to give up and be shot somewhere between here and town?"

Nuck grew red around the temples, a strange phenomenon for the man. "Don't judge me by your standards, Boadley. I guarantee a safe return and a safe trial."

"You guarantee it," Allan drawled. "But who guarantees your guarantee?"

Nuck let that lay. He pushed to another topic. "The rest of your crowd I ain't interested in—now. But I want them men of mine back. I want 'em now."

"You won't get them," Allan assured him. "That's my insurance. I might make this proposition, though. I'll give up to that warrant and go back with you. When the trial is finished, you'll get your men—if it's a fair trial. Moreover, the rest of our outfit will follow you into town to see me safe."

Nuck raised his head, plainly surprised at this sudden

turn. He had never expected Allan to give in so easily. Yet, to conceal his astonishment, he protested sullenly, "Won't do it. You got to deliver my men first. No other consideration."

"Don't push the thing too far," Allan warned. "Nothing in your warrant says anything about those men. You can't collect them and you can't find them. We stand on a par at the present time and we mean to stay that way until this scrape is ironed out."

"It won't be ironed out—" Nuck checked his temper. It had been on the point of betraying him. Allan perfectly understood what the man meant. It wouldn't be ironed out until all the Boadleys were dead. He grinned at his slack-lipped adversary.

"Guess you didn't expect to lose those men, did you, Nuck? That's one trump you haven't got. I'll go to town—but I'll be protected when I get there. And if I don't get there you can figure you're out sixteen good hands. And you can likewise figure on sudden demise for yourself."

Part of that was bluff; Allan well knew that neither he nor any of his party would injure the prisoners. It was only trading talk.

Nuck lowered his head and scratched the ground with the point of a twig. After a long silence he nodded his head. "That's agreed."

"I'll go back and tell the bunch."

Nuck rose. "No tricks now. I don't trust you."

"That cuts on two sides," Allan replied. He retreated, keeping an eye on Nuck until he was beyond decent revolver range. Swinging over the ledge, he found all of the crew standing by the cavern, guns drawn. They had been watching.

"Another election last night," Allan announced. "Nuck's sheriff again. Got a warrant for my arrest. Murder of Old Pierre. I made a dicker with him to give up. But we keep the prisoners and you boys follow me in to see it's a square deal."

"It won't wash," Snass objected. "Nope, that's out."

"What else?" Allan countered. "We can't stay like this forever. And we've got to eat. Anyhow, we're as strong as they are. We can risk any phony trial they might pull."

"They'll convict you," Strick said. "Sure as shooting."

"Let's cross that bridge when we come to it. Right now we can't afford to buck the law. Nuck's the law. He can get a posse big enough to wipe us out. If we manage to run for it we're the same as abandoning everything we own in this county. See how it works? He's half hoping we'll fight for just that little item."

"You won't ever reach town," Snass said.

"They won't do cold murder."

The girl broke in. "Nuck will." All the crowd looked at her in astonishment. And the attention confused her. Still, she held her ground. "You ought not to do it. Why not agree to meet Nuck in town and surrender there?"

"That's sound," Snass approved.

But Allan shook his head. "I know Nuck. He'd consider that a refusal to surrender and go ahead with this exterminating process. Anyhow, I want to be along with his party to see they don't try to ambush you. If they start such a trick I can make one good bellow before they gag me. All right. It's agreed. I'm going down. You wait about fifteen minutes and follow."

He got his horse and swung to the saddle. It seemed to him his brothers were about to stop him, so he shook his head several times and rode off the ledge. Nuck was there to meet him and had a gun out. Allan reached for his own piece, reversed it, and handed it over. Of a sudden Nuck's whole face was a-glitter with emotion. "Now, damn you, move ahead! And the first break on your part is your last!"

"Don't get rough," Allan cautioned. "You're dealing all cards off the top of the deck, understand?"

"Go ahead. Go ahead, dammit."

Allan reached the bottom of the canyon, rode on into the saplings and suddenly came face to face with the assembled Champifer faction. They were strung in a semicircle, holding to their horses, and they inspected him narrowly, with so complete and so ominous a silence that Allan experienced a faint touch of fore-boding. Luke Only was grinning through a villainous looking stubble. Luke's thin jaws worked up and down, and Allan saw the malevolent, sardonic satisfaction imprinted on the tight, up-curving muscles of the man's lips.

"Let's go," Nuck growled. "We got him."

"How about the other boys?" Luke Only demanded.

"Leave it to me," Nuck said. "Come on, let's go."

The party mounted and swung into a line. Nuck motioned for Allan to go ahead. Luke Only took the lead and circled through the timber. This was the trail along which Allan had brought his men previously, and once, through a vista of the pines, he saw his party slowly coming down the slope of the canyon wall. Nuck likewise saw this and barked savagely at Luke, "For God's sake, get along!"

Their speed increased. For the best part of an hour they cruised thus, fording an occasional creek, turning across some rugged defile. The undergrowth thinned. Nuck spoke again. "Get off the trail and swing west."

"It's shortest this way," said Luke Only.

"Swing west, I'm telling you!"

They left the established trail. Nuck pointed to one of his men in the rear. "Drop back and smooth over our tracks where we pulled off."

"From the top of the deck, Nuck," Allan reminded. "Deal them from the top."

Nuck stared at him. The man's eyes were turning blood shot. Allan had once seen a cougar crouched on a rock ledge, about to spring on a young colt. Just before the spring, the cougar had worked himself into a silent rage, lashing his tail from side to side. He recalled the scene now; Nuck was goading himself to the killing pitch. The detour from the main trail was to throw the rest of the Boadleys off scent. Probably it was Nuck's intention to work a double treachery—to kill and to ambush in the same morning.

It wasn't imagination. Allan had a plain inner

warning. Always in the face of unseen danger he had been warned by a feeling of cold followed by prickly heat along the base of his neck. It came now.

They were at a dead gallop, threading the sparse pines. Presently they arrived at the very edge of the desert. Nuck raised his arm and the column came to a swirling halt. Nuck motioned to his father and the two of them moved out of earshot. Presently another of the Champifer men and Little William tailed after. Nuck grumbled irritably at this intrusion, but both new-comers held their ground. Allan watched them grimly; they were talking about him. At odd intervals Nuck's head bobbed his way. Luke was staring at the ground and it seemed to Allan that the older one's face settled. Little William sat like a ramrod and held his peace, but the fourth man, who had no Champifer blood in him, shook his head from side to side and spat a phrase out of his mouth as if in plain disgust. "No, I'll be damned if I stand for it! No, no, no!"

"Who in hell asked your opinion!" Nuck stormed.

"I'm giving it whether you want it or not!" the puncher shouted. His voice dropped, but he was talking so fast Nuck couldn't interrupt. When he had finished, both Luke and Little William seemed to side with him. Nuck swore bitterly and spurred back to the column. "Come on, come on!" They galloped into the desert.

Nuck raced ahead of the party. Allan was aware of a horseman coming beside him. It was the protesting puncher. The man dropped an eyelid, muttering, "Be

122

careful. Don't make no hasty moves."

Eastward, Allan saw a train of dust. That would be his own party going on into town. Why hadn't they stopped to pick up the trail? Nuck swept down an arroyo, the rest following. Here, cut off from view, this half-crazed, blood-lusting Champifer stopped again and motioned for his men to draw up. "Leave that Boadley back there," he said.

Allan shook his head. They were giving him plenty of room to make a run. The old Mexican stunt. "Not now, Nuck. I've read about it in story books."

Nuck swung his horse and came back. He leaned far out of his saddle, breathing hard. "You trying to outfox me, huh? Playing double! What's that dust kicking up yonder for? It's your men beating us into town! I told you I'd stand for no tricks!"

"If you'd stuck to the trail," Allan countered, "you'd be there by now. Don't try it, kid. You'd better string into Grail with me alive and kicking or you'll be crated and sunk six feet below. Fifty-fifty now."

Nuck backed his horse off five yards. He dropped the reins and rested both arms on his hips. Luke Only angrily broke in. "Cut that out, Nuck. We don't have to. There's a better way."

Nuck weaved his head from side to side. "Mind your own business. I made an agreement with this gent and he's busted it. He's got us boxed and by God—"

The protesting puncher moved beside Allan and was about to speak. Nuck motioned him back. Allan gathered his muscles. This was Nuck's affair; the rest seemed half-hearted about a cold killing. Well, he might make a decent try of it. He dropped his left heel gently and waited. The horse stirred beneath him, feeling the prick of the spur. The sunshine seemed to grow dimmer. With his eyes half closed he saw only Nuck Champifer's twisted and cruel face warped and congested by passion. Allan's nerves seemed to desert him. Incuriously he noted a small dead white patch run along Nuck's upper lip. And there was the smell of sage in the air and the sky was a deep, deep blue. A thrumming of many horses!

The Champifer partisans snapped around in the direction of the noise. Over the arroyo's rim poured men and horses; over and down until they were directly facing the waiting feudists. Allan's skipping eyes saw T. Ulysses Gove foremost. Behind was Herod Ames, purveyor of bonded beverages. These were the townsmen, missing since the early part of the fight two nights ago.

"Who are you?" Nuck snapped, pointing a fist at Gove.

Gove announced his bare name in a melancholy voice. His attention lighted on Allan, but according to his roundabout habit, he gave no sign of recognition. "Saw you boys from the trees. Thought we'd go on to town with you. No objections?"

Herod Ames refused to wait upon an answer. "What you gents got Allan Boadley there for? Where's his gun?"

"You were the gents that ambushed us the other

night," Nuck said. "You'd ought to be took care of right now."

"Mebbe, but *you* won't do it," was Ames's belligerent reply. "I'm asking you a question."

"If you want to know," Nuck growled, "I'll say I'm taking him to jail on a warrant. It may be news to you I'm sheriff."

T. Ulysses Gove staved off Herod Ames. His was the very essence of polite formality. "Such being your official capacity, Sheriff. I'm glad to see you keeping the gent from any illegal harm. We'll ride along, I take it."

"Where'd you come from?" Nuck asked. "What's your business in this affair?"

"Me?" Gove seemed apologetic. "I'm just riding through from the next county. Met your fellow townsmen up in the forest."

"Let's ride and cut this palaver," Ames said.

"Go ahead," Nuck said, turning surly.

"No," was Ames's significant answer, "we'll ride behind. Never do to raise dust in a sheriff's face."

Luke Only muttered something to Nuck. The Champifer crew got in motion, passing the townsmen. Allan thought he saw Gove wink mournfully as he rode by that extraordinary gentleman.

One hour later he was in Grail City's battered jail and the town was a ferment once more with the factions. The august court was about to convene in a special session. Already the legal machinery had begun to operate. For the trials in Grail County were few, and justice, whatever its tortuous path and its obscure ending, was swift.

7.   The cards fall wrong

Judge Addis was on the bench, listening to Ralph Torger. The judge was a solemn slothful man whose venerable whiskers concealed a soiled white collar hitched to a felt shirt. Long ago the judge had read a little of Blackstone—when Blackstone represented the ultimate in common law—and had once been able to render a free translation of Caesar's Commentaries. On the desk before him ranged three volumes coated with dust: the session laws of the state, the annual report of the Stockmen's Association and a brand book, all of which he impartially ignored. Grail County elected him term after term. There was never any opposition; save for Ralph Torger who was prosecuting attorney, no other lawyer lived in the county. Grail seldom took to the law. Petty misdemeanors went unnoticed and capital offenses rarely reached court. There hadn't been a grand jury in fifteen years, a writ of any kind was almost unknown, and civil cases were ordinarily argued by the involved parties on a catch-as-catch-can plan and decided by the judge with due regard to political affiliations and family influence. Still, Grail seemed satisfied. He was the only one in that desert region who looked anything like a judge and he was too old to be shot at by the losing litigants. The right of appeal from his decisions existed, of course, but the county hadn't been educated to that finesse. A case important enough to warrant such procedure either was settled on the high desert or else the appeal was to a more popular and infinitely less judicial kind of judge.

As for Torger, he was a middle-aged man living on the Champifer side of town. He made a living mainly from a feed store and a job press, but occasionally he drew a will, assayed ore, auctioned, or traded in horses. As a prosecutor he ran true to the type, possessing a bulldog face and a voice that could lash and cut like a knife. At present he was explaining why he had arbitrarily filled the jury seats with twelve Champifer townsmen.

"Trials cost money to the county," Torger said, addressing Addis. "Sooner we dispose of this the less the taxpayers are out. If it please the court, I suggest the defendant be made to put his questions collectively to the jury and not to any single one. I am satisfied with the panel, knowing them all to be honest men who will carefully weigh the evidence and reach a decision upon its merits only."

"So decided," Addis droned. "Mister Boadley, you may question them. My policy has always been to give a juror all benefit of doubt. I won't excuse any except on very serious grounds of prejudice."

Allan tilted back his chair, grinning. His three brothers sat beside him and the Boadley crew were ranked along the wall. Across from them stood the Champifers, somber and watchful.

"It's your case and it's your jury," Allan said, speaking to Torger. "Why should I ask them questions? I know what the answers would be before I asked. None of those gentlemen has any bias in the case. None of them know anything about the facts of it. Their minds are as blank as a piece of paper. It's as fair a jury as could be collected—in Grail."

Torger glowered at Allan. "You accept 'em?" he snapped.

Allan's attention passed along the twelve true and impartial citizens. They were Champifer townsmen, all. They subscribed to the Champifer code. They were owned by Champifer clan, body and breeches. But on the very end of the double row sat one man whose fat substance and sleepy face Allan carefully avoided. It was Shoe Jim.

"I accept them," Allan said.

"Rise to be sworn in," Addis mumbled, and the jury rose.

Susan Champifer was in the courtroom, sitting on a foremost chair. The Boadleys had brought her back to town and she had immediately gone to a room in the hotel. Once, before the trial opened, both Nuck and Luke had called to see her and she had refused to let them in. Nuck watched her with a sidling, morose glance. The judge slid through the oath and turned again to Torger. "All right, call your witnesses."

"I wish to present a piece of paper which should be marked as Exhibit A," Torger said, holding it in his hand.

"How many exhibits you got?" Addis wanted to know.

"We have two—which is all we need."

"We'll dispense with formalities," Addis said, waving a pudgy hand. "Read it to the court."

So Torger read the spurious challenge Nuck Champifer had written and placed in the collar of Old Pierre after he had killed the man. *"All Champifers take care. The peace is ended. This is some pay for killing Lone Star. And you'll pay more."*

"Signature to that?" Addis queried.

"None," Torger replied. "But I will show it to be Allan Boadley's handwriting and for that purpose will now call a citizen of this town who is familiar with the defendant's penmanship. Joe Gallon, step to the witness box."

Joe Gallon ambled forward from the crowd, raised his hand and took the oath. Gallon was another Champifer townsman, his profession being carpentry. It made no difference that Allan had never trafficked with this individual or any other Champifer merchant. It was a Champifer trial; therefore what did it matter? Gallon took the note, studied it with apparent care and cleared his throat. "I can answer a question," he said.

"Who's writing is that?"

"Allan Boadley's. Seen it many a time. He's wrote me several letters about lumber et cetery."

"That's all," Torger snapped. He turned to Allan. "Your witness."

"No questions," Allan drawled. There was a stir in

the courtroom. Snass whispered huskily to Allan. Susan turned with an anxious glance. But Allan was smiling again. "No questions," he repeated. "I'm only an interested spectator here."

"You're something more than that," Torger retorted. "You're the guilty party. You'll hang. Better put up a decent show while you can."

"Hell!" said Snass.

Addis shook his head. "Cut out the profanity. I'll do all the needed swearing in this chamber."

"They ain't words enough in your grammar to supply all the needed profanity, you old duck," Snass told him.

"Another allusion like that and you go out," Addis warned. "Proceed with the trial. This jury ain't got all day to sit here. And I got to drive twenty miles for supper."

Snass fell to an expressive silence. He spat at the cuspidor and sprinkled the august prosecutor's leg, at which Torger grew vehement. "Some men here ain't got no delicacy and their aim is horrible poor. I will next call Cal Levering."

Cal Levering, under oath, testified that on the night of the killing, he happened to be riding the desert. He heard the shot and he saw a horseman later heading toward town. Couldn't see the fellow's face but he found a bandanna on the ground beside Old Pierre's body. Old Pierre had torn it from the murderer's neck. The bandanna was next produced by Torger.

"That it?"

"Yeah."

"Do you know to whom it belongs?"

"Uhuh. Allan Boadley's initials is on it in black ink."

"Your witness," Torger said, turning to Allan.

But Allan was asking no questions that day. He said so. The courtroom stirred again and Nuck looked around with a tight, worried glance. Snass got up and, followed by Strick, left the room. Out on the street he solaced himself with a little tobacco. T. Ulysses Gove came ambling after. Gove observed the sky, the earth and all the many facets of nature. Presently he ventured a mild remark.

"Sort of illegal procedure," he said. "I'm accustomed to informality in my own county, but this here seems a leetle beyond the mark."

"Illegal, brother?" Snass snorted. "Hell, it's about as legal as anything else in Grail. It's their party, not ours. Ain't you acquainted with this country?"

"By reputation," Gove said. "Allan had better start entering some exceptions so's he can appeal."

"That dodo duck of a judge don't know what an exception is. He'd think it meant something personal. Oh, there'll be an appeal all right, all right." Snass looked somberly around him. "Ten cents worth of legality to cover forty dollars of crookedness. That's Grail. We're hell on formality here and it don't mean nothing."

"Then what's the use of going through with the trial?" Strick demanded. "It's crooked. We know it's crooked. They know we know it's crooked. That jury had a decision before they reached our side of the river."

"The answer is," Snass stated, "we ain't giving Sheriff Nuck any undue chance of establishing the rest of us as abetting a criminal, see? He could rig a posse and chase us all to hell and gone."

"We'll have to fight anyhow," Strick argued.

"Yeah, mebbe. We'll cross that bridge when we come to it. Them boys may get cold feet before the sun goes down." He stared at Gove. "Say, what happened to you the other night when we was jumping from building to building? Get lost?"

"I pulled stakes," Gove said. "Conservation is my motto. When a scrap gets too hot for me I skip. Always can come back again some other time. A dead man pulls no triggers."

"For a small geezer you got a powerful lot of ideas," Snass murmured. He wasn't sure whether he liked Gove or not.

"If I was you," Gove said, diffidently, "I believe I'd go right now and lock all doors in this town excepting them *you* want to duck into. Make the other party fight on the street."

Snass was about to answer when he heard sudden confusion rolling out of the courtroom. He went running into the place to find Susan Champifer on her feet, trying to speak. Torger was shouting, "Irrelevant— immaterial! I object, I object! Testimony is all in—too late for her to testify! Incompetent! I object!"

"Oh, bust him on the coco," Strick muttered.

Judge Addis alternately stroked his whiskers and pounded the desk with his gavel. "Objection sustained. The lady is out of order." The courtroom was suddenly swirling with protest and recrimination. Addis became perfectly still, his eyes darting across the scene. He reversed his position with nimbleness. "No, objection overruled. Take the chair, ma'am."

Allan was on his feet for the first time. Nobody heard what he said to Torger, so great was the uproar at the moment. But the prosecuting attorney turned flaming red of face and subsided. Allan towered over the man, a menacing figure, ablaze with the slow, hard wrath of his family. Then order came back to the room. The girl raised her hand and without prompting began to speak.

"All this is ridiculous. Allan Boadley didn't kill my father. I have proof of it. My father received a note from Allan Boadley that night. I saw the note. It asked my father to come in town for a meeting with Allan. He put the note in his pocket when he left. I saw my cousin Nuck riding after Dad. And later Nuck came back alone although he thought nobody had observed him. The next day we got word of my father's death. All the while I was suspicious and so—so that night I managed to get into Nuck's clothing. And I found Allan Boadley's note in Nuck's coat. He had taken it from my father. He killed my father!"

Nuck was on his feet, the words choking in his throat. "You lie! You damned jade!"

"Swallow that," Allan said, "or I'll knock you down. Swallow it!"

Judge Addis had risen and nearly fell over his desk. "Order, order! Mister Champifer, you'll kindly render apologies due the lady."

"Well, all right," Nuck muttered, yellow-faced. "But it's a lie."

"That's for the jury to decide," Addis said. "Now, ma'am, you got possession of the note?"

She held it in her hand. Torger reached for it with a sudden swift move. She drew away. "I'm not trusting you, Torger." She walked to the jury and gave it to the foremost man. And she watched it pass from hand to hand, never for an instant letting her attention waver. Shoe Jim was the last recipient. He handed it back to her. She walked to the judge's desk and laid it before him. "This trial's a mockery. That bandanna you introduced as belonging to Allan Boadley was never around his neck."

"So?" was Torger's biting interjection. "How does it come that you, a Champifer, can know so much about a Boadley?"

The witness chair stood raised a little above the floor of the room and thus she was a fair target for all. Hands locked in front of her, she seemed to be framing a reply that would carry conviction, that would sway the jury. Turning, her black eyes fell upon Allan and rested momentarily there. Allan's face seemed cut of bronze, bleak and sharp and cold. He had never seen a woman's eyes so strangely clear; and such was the power of them that he felt alternately humble and blazing proud.

"A woman who likes a man," she said, words carrying clearly across the hushed room, "would always notice what that man wore. I have seen Allan many times. That bandanna was blue. Allan never wears anything but a red neck piece."

Torger waved his hand at Allan in mock politeness. "Your witness."

"Come down, Susan," Allan said gently. He took her arm and saw her to a chair. Torger was addressing the jury. "I rest my case. It seems to me quite a clear and convincing case. As for the lady's testimony, I leave you to judge. But she admits she is fond of the defendant. Such being the case, her talk is to be taken with salt. That's all."

"Defendant," droned Judge Addis.

"Nothing to say," Allan said grimly.

"The jury will repair to the next room and reach a decision," Addis instructed. "I will observe that as it's getting late and I got to drive twenty miles, the jury should be some celerious in their report. Won't take time to go through the whole procedure as to evidence and hearsay and reasonable doubt. You boys have heard it before. Move out."

The courtroom settled down to a period of waiting. Addis retired. Snass rose and made his exit, casting a significant glance here and there. In response to that glance a half dozen punchers sifted into the street and stood around him. One by one he gave them a chore to do.

"Bill, go to the stables and stay there—no matter what happens. Ortley, you get to the second story

135

window of Markowitz's. Whitely and John, post your-selves by the jail. Neal, same at the hotel. Jake, you go back inside the courtroom and pass it around nobody's to move a finger till they catch my signal. That applies to all you boys. Hoof it."

T. Ulysses Gove emerged from the judicial sanctum and moved away.

"Where *you* going?" Snass inquired.

"To find a leetle shade," was Gove's cryptic reply.

Snass shook his head at the departing figure. A spear of grass'd cast enough shade for him, Snass thought. I don't make out the gent at all.

Somebody whistled. Strick was at the courtroom door beckoning, and Strick's eyes were glittering with excitement. "They're back." Snass moved inside with the deliberation of one who had nothing at all on his mind. The foreman of the jurors had risen.

"Got a verdict?" Addis inquired. Then he interrupted the foreman's reply long enough to address the audi-ence. "This atmosphere is some heated. I'm warning you. If they's got to be any shooting, do it outside. Won't tolerate no nonsense here."

It grew painfully silent. Robe Boadley stood with his back to the wall, husking the paper off a stick of gum, and his blue eyes wandered idly along the assembled Champifers. Strick had a tight smile on his face. Snass was never a hand to give vent to emotion. He sat beside the equally grave Allan, and his only concession to a possible emergency was to put on his hat in defiance of etiquette. Susan bent forward in her chair, white-lipped. Of all the crowd, she seemed to take it with the most concern.

The foreman cleared his throat. "No verdict. Jury couldn't agree."

It was as if the wind had passed across a field of wheat. Such was the rustle of expelled breath. To the Boadleys, who had expected conviction, it was a complete surprise—except to Allan. For the Champifers it came as a stunning shock. Nuck was yellow-white. Luke Only seemed to age and grow grayer. Torger ran a hand through his hair and snapped, "What was that?"

"Jury disagreed," the foreman repeated. And then, as if by a preconcerted arrangement, eleven of that jury turned and silently stared at Shoe Jim. The fat mender of shoes had his eyes half closed. He looked like an Oriental in repose. But he stood condemned, by that silent inspection of his compeers, as the only one who had refused to vote a Boadley to death.

"Case ended," Addis said hastily. "Court closed. Move out slowly."

The Champifers held to their places, not yet able to collect themselves out of their defeat. Allan took Susan by the arm and led her from the room. Shoe Jim came to life, stepped past Nuck toward the Boadleys. Nuck watched the man from narrowing lids. He made a slight downward motion of one hand. But Shoe Jim went on, unscathed, and presently all the Boadleys were in the hotel, jubilant yet watchful. Outside on the street, the opposite faction passed toward the bridge with an unnatural silence.

"Calm before a storm," Strick said. He turned to Allan. "So you had a little trick of your own? By Jim, you always got one trump somewhere. I never saw you beat."

Allan turned to Shoe Jim, who stood apart from the rest of the men. He walked over and put a hand across the fat one's shoulder. "Boys, this fellow has served us in a secret capacity for a good many years, and never a Champifer knew it. From now on he's an out and out Boadley. Does he get a drink?"

"Out of a silver cup!" Strick yelled.

"Ain't no silver cups in Grail City," put in the practical Snass.

"Shucks, I was speaking categorically—ain't that the word?"

Susan Champifer came down the stairway from her room, beckoning Allan. "Allan, I know my cousin. It isn't over yet. But—but I'm glad they failed to make that charge stick! And, Allan—whatever I said—you must forget."

"How could I be forgetting?" Allan muttered.

A touch of color came to her cheeks. And even in her anxiety there was a trace of humor, a stirring of something far back in her eyes. "Remember what I once told you. A man may never, never take advantage of a woman."

Bill Baines slid through the hotel doorway, issuing a sharp and gritty warning. "The three Champifers is coming across the bridge. Luke, Little William and Nuck, all by themselves. Walking plenty serious."

"I'm going out to talk with them," said the girl, But Allan shook his head. His arm barred her. "Not now. They never listened to you. They wouldn't this minute. Don't you see? This is the last play. It's their last stand. Even their crew has gone back. They're meaning for me to meet them."

"But you won't go!"

He had turned about. "All right. Snass and Robe, you come with me. We'll go out there."

"I'll trail along," Strick said gruffly.

"No. We'll make it fifty-fifty."

Susan took hold of Allan's shoulders and pulled him around. "Allan, you won't—"

"I gave you a promise once," Allan said. "I'll let him draw first. This range war is about to end."

"I won't take that promise!" she cried. "I know my cousin—"

Snass touched his gun once and squared his shoulders. Robe, without a trace of expression on his brown face, moved into line. Strick swore softly as Allan joined them. And then they were out of the door and moving slowly to the very middle of the dusty street; Susan saw them wheel, elbow to elbow, and she had a clear view of them for a moment before they passed on down toward the bridge. Three stalwart men with the last rays of the evening sun touching the fringe of their yellow hair and throwing a shadow across their faces. Those were honest faces, set now as she imagined they would be set in death—without emotion, bleak, cheek muscles ridged against the brown skin. Allan's hat was tilted rakishly and his neck piece fluttered a little. They passed out of sight.

"Why don't you go out there!" Susan exclaimed.

But the crew stood still. Strick shook his head. "It's their play now." And he went to the counter, picked up the pen and began to write meaningless names on the register. He threw a single toneless command over his shoulder. "Bill, stand in the doorway and watch. If any of their crew join in—"

It seemed to the girl that the world had stopped revolving, that all things came to a stand. She had the queer, giddy feeling that time had ceased. She was surrounded by a vacuum and in this vacuum she couldn't think. She felt nothing, she no longer drew breath. It was as if she were transfixed for eternity. Across the room she saw the men and they too had ceased to live, they too were frozen. One brown face ran into another, all drawn and blurred. Strick whirled like a top and threw his pen as far as he could.

"No, by God!"

Gunfire rolled along the street in short staccato waves. She tried to count them and got as far as three before the conflicting bursts put her off the track. It rose to a crackling climax and sheered to nothing. And then again that oppressive, fearful silence. Bill Baines turned from the door, his lips drawn back, some kind of emotion printed on his face. But she couldn't see what it was—he seemed that blurred to her. Another figure came to the door, both hands stretched wide to grip the supporting boards. Blood

140

ran freely down and his holster was empty.

"It's over," Allan said. "It's all over. And I'm the only one that's left."

Strick ran across the room and shielded his brother from sight. Allan seemed to be crying, gripped by some terrific spasm. Strick turned a savage face to the crew. "Get out of here. Get out, you fools!"

Dusk came again to Grail and with dusk came peace. The glow of lights ran along the dusty thoroughfare and glinted across the sluggish stream. Once more the chieftain of the Boadleys met the chieftain of the Champifers on the bridge.

"I have let off half my crew," Susan said. "They were the gunmen. All who are left are loyal to me. There will be no more war, Allan. There won't even be a truce. It's peace."

"I'll send a boy up to bring down those fifteen fellows we've been keeping prisoners," Allan said.

"There will have to be another election," Susan remarked thoughtfully. "You will run—and I shall instruct all my men to vote for you."

"I'm through."

"Who is a better man to keep the peace, Allan Boadley? You will run."

"The river's dry down by the sinks," Allan suggested. "I'd better send a man to patrol my side of the fence."

"I shall do the same."

"One man," Allan said, "would be plenty."

"I had thought so."

"And," Allan continued, "I figured I'd be the one to

ride for the Boadleys. Tomorrow night about seven or eight o'clock."

Her hand dropped lightly on his shoulder. He heard the barest whisper. "Allan—I'll be there to meet you." Then her horse drummed off the bridge. He retreated, seeing the Champifers ride slowly from town. In the rear of the procession was a wagon bearing a canvas covered burden. Allan passed a hand across his face. It cost a price, he thought. God only knows it cost a price. But it's ended. Dead as cold ashes, never to rise again. How can it rise when this county will be one range instead of two?

A wisp of a figure emerged from the dusk. It was T. Ulysses Gove, accoutered with the trappings of travel. "You got that warrant for Nuck Champifer still in your pocket, Boadley?"

"Yes."

"Tear it up. Glad I didn't have to serve it. Oh, I'd of served it if it came to such a pass. Only I take my time and let Providence work its mysterious ways. Ain't it better for the man to be dead? Maybe we'd have convicted him, maybe we wouldn't of. Justice is devious. And all my county is out is the price of seven-eight meals. Cheap and effective." He paused to collect some last farewell sentiment. "It's a short life, Boadley. You'll be sheriff many a time. Take your leisure. Don't follow no story book ways. What ain't done today can always wait for tomorrow. It takes a long pole to catch a crook and life is sure a sweet thing when it runs out of you through a bullet hole. Ever comes a time you need help, lemme know. So long."

He vanished. Allan sent a hail into the darkness. "So long, Gove." The dining room of the hotel was a-clatter with dishes. Markowitz stood in the doorway of his store, smoking a cigar. Allan passed along to the hotel porch and sat down, looking at the stars so remote. A soft night wind struck his cheeks. Grail County had bought peace.

Center Point Publishing
600 Brooks Road ● PO Box 1
Thorndike ME 04986-0001 USA

(207) 568-3717

US & Canada:
1 800 929-9108